The Last Knights Templar

THE LAST KNIGHTS TEMPLAR

First edition. December 12, 2024.

ISBN: 979-8227295743

Written by Antonio Templar.

Dedication

To the indomitable spirit of the Knights Templar, whose unwavering faith and courage in the face of adversity

continue to inspire awe and wonder centuries later. This story is a testament to their enduring legacy, a tribute to their unwavering brotherhood, and a celebration of their valiant struggle to protect the sacred trust entrusted to them. It is dedicated to those who have dared to dream of hidden histories, to those who have sought truth in the face of persecution, and to those who cherish the echoes of faith and courage that resonate through the corridors of time. May their unwavering commitment to their beliefs serve as a beacon of hope and inspiration for generations to come, reminding us that even in the darkest of times, the light of faith and the strength of brotherhood can prevail. This narrative, woven from the threads of history and imagination, is offered as a small token of gratitude for their sacrifices, a humble attempt to capture the essence of their perilous journey and the enduring strength of their spirit, a testament to the resilience of the human spirit in the face of unimaginable odds. Their unwavering dedication to their beliefs and their unwavering commitment to their sacred mission serve as an enduring testament to the power of faith and brotherhood. May this story serve as a beacon of hope, inspiring us all to face our own challenges with unwavering courage and determination.

Preface

The whispers of the Knights Templar, once a formidable order guarding the Holy Land, continue to echo through the annals of history. Their abrupt and brutal demise, shrouded in mystery and fuelled by accusations of heresy, left behind a legacy of intrigue and speculation that persists to this day.

This novel delves into the heart of this enigma, drawing upon historical accounts and weaving a fictional narrative that explores the possible fate of the last remaining Templars after the devastating papal decree of 1307. Their flight from the Holy Land, their perilous voyage across the ocean, and their struggle to establish a new sanctuary in the unforgiving wilderness of Nova Scotia form the backbone of this tale. It's a journey fraught with peril, testing their faith, their brotherhood, and their very survival. We will witness their cunning ingenuity in constructing a hidden vault to safeguard their precious relics, the booby traps meticulously designed to deter any who would dare to steal their sacred treasures, and their constant vigilance against those who seek to uncover their secrets. Beyond the thrilling adventure, this story aims to explore the complexities of faith, betrayal, and the enduring strength of human resilience in the face of relentless persecution. The clash between the Templars' commitment to their sacred beliefs and the political machinations of the time provides a rich backdrop against which this adventure unfolds. The desolate beauty of the Nova Scotian landscape serves as a stark yet fitting stage for this dramatic struggle for survival, underscoring the isolation and determination of these courageous knights. The reader is invited to journey alongside these courageous knights, to experience the hardships they endure, the bonds of brotherhood they forge, and the profound faith that sustains them as they navigate the treacherous waters of survival, betrayal, and the ever-present shadow of their past.

Introduction

In the year of our Lord 1307, a dark shadow fell upon the Knights Templar, an order once revered for their unwavering devotion to Christendom and their valiant defense of the Holy Land. Pope Clement V, bowing to political pressures and fueled by unfounded accusations, issued a devastating decree, outlawing the Templars and condemning them to persecution. This act shattered the world of these brave knights, forcing them to flee the lands they had sworn to protect. This novel follows the harrowing journey of a small band of surviving Templars, who, rather than surrendering to their fate, embark on a desperate flight, carrying with them precious holy relics – symbols of their faith and their legacy. Their escape from the Holy Land is a perilous undertaking, a race against time and relentless pursuers. Their eventual arrival on the shores of Nova Scotia marks the beginning of a new chapter, a struggle for survival in the unforgiving wilderness of a new land. The harsh climate and the

unfamiliar landscape pose significant challenges, testing their resourcefulness and their unwavering faith. They

embark on a secret mission: to conceal their sacred treasures deep within the earth, creating a hidden sanctuary protected by ingenious booby traps, a testament to their unwavering determination to preserve their heritage. This is not merely a tale of adventure and survival, but a profound exploration of faith, brotherhood, and the enduring strength of the human spirit in the face of adversity. We will delve into the intricate relationships between these courageous knights, their struggles to maintain unity and faith amid betrayal and despair, and their interactions with the indigenous population of their new homeland. The narrative unfolds against a backdrop of historical accuracy, intertwining factual events with compelling fictional elements to create a thrilling and suspenseful journey that will captivate readers. Prepare to be transported to 14th-century Jerusalem and the rugged landscapes of Nova Scotia, as you bear witness to the epic struggle of the last Templars to protect their legacy and their faith amidst the darkness and the relentless pursuit of their enemies. Their story will test the boundaries of courage, brotherhood, and faith, leaving you breathless until the very end.

Shadow of the Edict

The midday sun beat down on the cobbled streets of Jerusalem, casting long shadows from the ancient walls.

Within the Temple Mount, a hush fell over the usually

bustling courtyard of the Knights Templar's preceptory. Sir Geoffroi de Charny, his face etched with a grim

determination, stood before his assembled brethren, a

parchment clutched tightly in his hand. The air crackled with a tension so thick it could be cut with a sword. This was no ordinary meeting; this was a gathering forged in the crucible of impending doom.

The parchment, sealed with the papal signet, contained the decree that would shatter their world – Pope Clement V's edict, outlawing the Order of the Poor Fellow-Soldiers of Christ and of the Temple of Solomon. The words, stark and brutal, painted a grim picture: arrest, imprisonment, and, for many, a fiery death at the stake. The accusations – heresy, idolatry, sodomy – were vicious lies, yet the weight of the Pope's authority was inescapable. The whispers had been circulating for months, carried on the wind from Europe, but now, the official confirmation struck them with the force of a hammer blow.

A collective gasp rippled through the assembled knights. Disbelief warred with a chilling realization of the immediate danger. Years of unwavering service to the Church, of defending Christendom in the Holy Land, were reduced to ashes by a single stroke of a pen. The faces of these hardened warriors, men who had stared death in the eye countless times on the battlefields, were pale with shock. Sir Geoffroi, a man known for his unwavering resolve, felt a tremor of fear run down his spine. He had seen many battles, endured countless sieges, but this was a different kind of war, a war fought not with swords and shields, but with whispers and deceit.

The initial silence was broken by a surge of angry murmurs, a torrent of disbelief and outrage. Accusations of betrayal flew, fingers pointed at unseen enemies within the Church itself. But Geoffroi raised his hand, silencing the chaotic outburst with a commanding gesture. His voice, though strained, resonated with the authority of his rank and the steely resolve that had always characterized him. "Silence!" he roared, his voice echoing through the courtyard. "We are Templars. We do not succumb to panic. We adapt. We

survive."

His words, though intended to instill courage, did little to mask the gravity of their situation. The once-proud Order, a bulwark against the Saracens, was now hunted, its very existence threatened. The immediate task was not to mourn their loss, but to ensure their survival and protect the sacred relics entrusted to their care. They had to flee, and they had to do so swiftly and secretly.

The next few hours were a blur of frantic activity. A council of war convened, each knight contributing their expertise and experience. The most precious relics – fragments of the True Cross, a piece of the Holy Grail, the legendary Spear of Destiny – were carefully selected for transport. A clandestine inventory was taken, their spiritual treasures prioritized above all else. Years spent defending these sacred objects, believing in their protection, were all going to be put to the test. The weight of the task was immense, the knowledge that their actions could determine the future of Christianity. They couldn't afford to fail.

The question of their escape route dominated the discussions. The sea offered the only viable path, a perilous journey fraught with uncertainties. Saladin's forces, though not yet aware of the Papal decree's full impact, still presented a significant threat. Their movements had to be stealthy, their departure swift and silent as the shadow of the night. Each knight had a role, meticulously assigned, demonstrating years of training and understanding their roles.

Under the cloak of darkness, the Templars began their escape. The sacred relics, carefully concealed in specially constructed containers, were loaded onto a waiting ship. The journey was fraught with danger, the sea a tempestuous beast threatening to swallow them whole. Storms raged, testing the strength of the vessel and the courage of its passengers. But the Templars, seasoned sailors as well as warriors, held fast, their unwavering faith a guiding light in the midst of the darkness. Each wave that crashed against the hull, each gust of wind that threatened to capsize their vessel, only served to strengthen their resolve. They were not merely escaping; they were carrying the very essence of Christendom to a new sanctuary.

Days blurred into weeks as they braved the relentless onslaught of the sea. They suffered shortages of food and water. Seasickness plagued many, and wounds festered untreated. But they endured, their shared purpose a stronger bond than any physical hardship. The horrors of the sea only made the distant land, their new haven, even more enticing.

Finally, after what felt like an eternity, land appeared on the horizon. The rugged coast of Nova Scotia, a wilderness unknown to most Europeans, beckoned. The ship limped into a hidden cove, the Knights Templar, battered but unbroken, stepping onto the shores of a new world. The weight of the decree, the persecution, and the arduous journey lay behind them. Their future, however, was as uncertain as the vast wilderness that now surrounded them. The shadow of the Papal edict still loomed large, but so did the flicker of hope – the hope of a new beginning, a new sanctuary to protect the sacred relics and the legacy of the Knights Templar. Their journey was far from over. The real struggle, the fight for survival and the preservation of their faith, was only just beginning.

Gathering the Relics

The air in the preceptory, thick with the scent of incense and the weight of unspoken fears, buzzed with hushed

conversations. Sir Geoffroi, his gaze sweeping over the assembled Knights, felt the familiar ache of responsibility press down on him. The Papal decree was not merely a sentence; it was a death knell, a chilling premonition of the fires that awaited them in Europe. Their only recourse was escape, a desperate flight to a land beyond the reach of Philip the Fair's vengeful grasp. But escape meant more than merely fleeing; it meant safeguarding the sacred trust bequeathed to the Order – the relics.

He cleared his throat, the sound echoing in the cavernous hall. "Brothers," he began, his voice low but resolute, "the time for deliberation is past. Our sanctuary in the Holy Land is lost. We must embark on a perilous journey, carrying with us the most precious relics of our Order, those entrusted to our keeping for centuries."

A murmur rippled through the assembled Knights. The very air seemed to vibrate with the weight of their sacred burden.

For generations, the Templars had guarded these artifacts, symbols of their faith and unwavering commitment to Christendom. Their loss would be a devastating blow, a catastrophic event that could shake the foundations of Christendom itself. The question was not

if

they should transport these relics, but
how

.

Brother Thomas, a scholar and scribe of considerable renown, stepped forward. "Sir Geoffroi," he said, his voice trembling slightly, "the task is daunting. We must identify which relics are of paramount importance, those whose loss would be most keenly felt by the Church."

Geoffroi nodded, his gaze settling on the meticulously crafted inventory. It was a testament to centuries of painstaking preservation, a catalogue of sacred objects

imbued with immense spiritual significance. The True Cross fragment, a tiny splinter of the wood upon which Christ was crucified, was undeniably the most crucial. Its loss would send shockwaves through the Christian world, questioning the very essence of their faith. Then there was the Holy Lance, supposedly the spear that pierced the side of Christ, a relic believed to possess miraculous healing powers. Its disappearance would be met with equal outrage and

disbelief.

A heated debate ensued. The Knights were not mere

soldiers; they were devout men of faith, each possessing a deep reverence for these sacred objects. Some argued for the inclusion of the Shroud of Turin, despite its questionable authenticity according to certain scholars. Others championed the preservation of the numerous smaller relics, the countless fragments of saints' bones, and fragments of clothing allegedly worn by the apostles.

Geoffroi listened patiently, his keen mind weighing the merits of each argument. He had to strike a balance between the historical and religious significance of each relic and the practicality of transporting them across the vast expanse of ocean to the unknown shores of Nova Scotia.

"Brothers," he declared finally, "we cannot carry everything.

Our mission is to safeguard the most important relics. The True Cross fragment and the Holy Lance are non-negotiable.

Their significance is too profound to risk."

He paused, his eyes locking with Brother Thomas. "We also take the Crown of Thorns," he added, his voice firm. "It symbolizes the suffering of Christ, a poignant reminder of our faith's sacrifice. It shall not be lost to the flames of persecution."

The choice was agonizing. Each relic left behind represented a loss, a part of their heritage that might be irrevocably lost to history. Yet, prudence dictated that they could only carry what could be concealed, transported, and protected in their new, precarious existence.

The next few days were a flurry of activity. The Knights meticulously prepared the relics for transport, wrapping them in layers of fine linen and concealing them within specially constructed containers. These weren't simple chests; they were ingenious creations, designed to withstand the rigors of a sea voyage and offer a degree of protection against theft or discovery. Secret compartments, false bottoms, and hidden locks were incorporated into their design, reflecting the Templar's long-standing expertise in safeguarding their treasures.

The most important relics were further secured within a larger, intricately designed coffer. This main container was itself placed within a false-bottomed cart, designed to blend seamlessly with everyday supplies and provisions. The cart was meant to be inconspicuous, its contents appearing as nothing more than mundane equipment and provisions needed for their long journey.

Meanwhile, others were busy with preparations for their departure. A ship was secured, a sturdy vessel, though not a grand galleon of the Royal Navy. It was a smaller ship, chosen for its maneuverability and ability to navigate the treacherous waters ahead. Provisions were collected, supplies were checked and double-checked. There were few luxuries; their focus was on survival. Every inch of space was utilized, every ounce of weight carefully considered.

Secret messages were prepared and distributed among a select few trusted contacts in Europe. These messages served not only as a testament to their existence but also as a beacon of hope for other surviving Templars, a signal that a refuge remained. The exact location of their new haven remained undisclosed, a closely guarded secret meant to be unveiled only to those deemed worthy.

As the sun set on Jerusalem, casting a long, somber shadow over the Temple Mount, the Knights Templar gathered for a final prayer. The air was heavy with solemnity, a poignant farewell to the city that had been their home for centuries. Tears were shed, vows were renewed, and a collective prayer for guidance and protection was offered.

The departure was clandestine, under the cover of darkness.

The small ship slipped away silently, leaving behind the chaos and persecution of Europe. Ahead lay the vast

uncertainty of the open ocean and the unknown wilderness of Nova Scotia. But within the hold of their ship, nestled among the seemingly innocuous supplies, lay the precious relics of their Order, entrusted to the last remaining Knights Templar. Their journey had begun – a desperate race against time, against enemies both seen and unseen, to safeguard their sacred treasures and the legacy of their fallen brethren.

The weight of their mission pressed upon them, but so did the unwavering conviction that their faith, and the relics entrusted to them, would survive. The future was uncertain, but their commitment to their sacred duty remained absolute. The perilous journey, a testament to their faith and resilience, had begun. The fate of the Knights Templar, and the future of Christendom itself, hung in the balance.

A Secret Departure

The flickering lamps of the Jerusalem preceptory cast long, dancing shadows as the Knights Templar made their final preparations. The air, heavy with the scent of woodsmoke and the unspoken dread of imminent betrayal, crackled with a nervous energy. Sir Geoffroi, his face etched with lines of weariness and grim determination, oversaw the loading of their small vessel, the

Sea Serpent

. Each crate and barrel was carefully inspected, its contents ostensibly mundane –supplies for a long voyage – but concealing within their innocuous exteriors the priceless relics of their Order. The Ark of the Covenant, a miniature replica painstakingly crafted over centuries, nestled amongst sacks of flour; the Holy Grail, disguised as an intricately carved wine cask, rested near barrels of salted fish. Each item, a tangible piece of their history, represented the enduring faith of generations of Templars, a faith now brutally threatened.

The departure was shrouded in secrecy, a clandestine

operation orchestrated with the precision born of years spent defending the Holy Land. Under the cover of a moonless night, the

Sea Serpent

, small and nimble, slipped away from the bustling port, avoiding the ever-vigilant eyes of Saladin's spies. The whispers of the Papal decree had reached even Jerusalem, fanning the flames of suspicion and animosity towards the Order. Geoffroi knew that lingering even an hour longer would risk exposure, and perhaps, capture or worse.

He cast one last, lingering glance towards the city, a silent farewell to the hallowed ground they were abandoning, the battlefields where their brethren had fallen, the sacred sites they had sworn to protect. A wave of melancholy washed over him, but it was quickly replaced by the steely resolve he needed to face the daunting journey ahead.

The Mediterranean was unforgiving. The

Sea Serpent

,
though seaworthy, was not built for long voyages. The

constant rocking of the waves, the relentless wind whipping across the deck, tested the limits of the Knights' endurance. Days bled into nights, marked only by the rhythmic creak of the ship's timbers and the tireless work of the men. Sea sickness ravaged some, leaving them weak and delirious, but the spirit of the remaining Templars remained unbroken. Their shared commitment to their sacred mission, the weight of their responsibility, held them together, a bond forged in the fires of persecution and fueled by unwavering faith.

Storms raged, threatening to swallow their small vessel whole. Waves crashed over the deck, soaking them to the bone, and the howling wind tore at the sails, threatening to rip them asunder. Geoffroi, his eyes fixed on the raging tempest, fought back the rising despair. The Knights,

weathered and exhausted, battled alongside him, their faces grim but resolute. They bailed out the water, repaired the tattered sails, and held on, clinging to the hope of reaching their destination. It was in these moments, amidst the fury of the elements, that their faith was truly tested. Prayers were muttered, hymns sung, their voices barely audible above the roar of the storm. Their reliance on God, and on each other, became their lifeline.

During the lulls between the storms, the Knights found moments of respite. They shared stories of their fallen

brethren, their voices hushed with reverence and sorrow. They reminisced about their past battles, their victories and defeats, their shared experiences forging a strong bond that transcended the hardship. The shared grief and the fear of what awaited them acted as a common, unspoken language among them. They knew they were running not just from the clutches of the King of France, but also from a possible fate worse than death: to abandon their sacred relics to the hands of those who would desecrate them. Their shared

determination served to reinforce their will, to strengthen their already fervent belief.

The rations dwindled, and hunger gnawed at their bellies, but they remained disciplined and stoic. They shared what little they had, each Knight sacrificing to ensure that their companions did not succumb to starvation. It was a

testament to the strength of their brotherhood, a bond that had endured centuries of war and now faced the ultimate test of survival. Their unity and their common objective became their compass guiding them through the treacherous waves.

These men had faced down Saracen armies, defended holy sites under siege, yet it was here on this fragile ship that their courage faced its true trial, away from the battlefields, alone in the vast and unforgiving expanse of the open sea.

Days turned into weeks, and finally, after what seemed an eternity, the land appeared on the horizon. The sight of the rugged, untamed coastline of Nova Scotia filled them with a mixture of relief and apprehension. They had survived the perilous journey, but their ordeal was far from over. Their arrival in the New World marked not an end, but a new beginning, a treacherous chapter in their long and arduous mission. The challenges that awaited them were many: the harsh climate, the uncharted wilderness, and the ever-present threat of discovery. They had escaped the immediate danger, but the shadow of the Papal decree still loomed large, its icy grip extending even to the distant shores of the New World. But as the

Sea Serpent

finally touched the sand, the Knights Templar, weary but resolute, stepped onto the shore, their eyes fixed on the task ahead: to protect their sacred trust, and the legacy of their Order, at any cost. The journey had been arduous, but it had also strengthened the bonds between these surviving Knights, a bond that would prove crucial in their struggle to survive and preserve the relics of the

Templar Order. The true fight was yet to begin. Their escape was merely the first step in a long and perilous quest. The desolate beauty of the Nova Scotian wilderness was now their sanctuary, but it was also a land that held both promise and peril in equal measure. Their arduous escape, though successful, had only bought them time, and the weight of their mission remained heavy on their hearts.

The Nova Scotia Shore

The

Sea Serpent

, battered and bruised from its transatlantic voyage, finally grounded itself on a small, secluded cove.

The men, gaunt and weary, stumbled onto the unfamiliar shore, their legs unsteady after weeks at sea. The air, sharp and invigorating after the close confines of the ship, carried the scent of pine and salt, a stark contrast to the dust and sweat of Jerusalem. Nova Scotia, a land unknown, promised both sanctuary and peril in equal measure.

Sir Geoffroi, his gaze scanning the rugged coastline, felt a surge of both relief and apprehension. They had evaded the papal hounds, but their journey was far from over. The vast, untamed wilderness stretched before them, a labyrinth of forests, mountains, and treacherous inlets. The task of finding a secure hiding place for their sacred relics felt insurmountable, a challenge as daunting as any battle they had faced in the Holy Land.

The first few days were spent in careful reconnaissance. Small scouting parties ventured into the dense forests, their movements silent and deliberate. They were hunters now, not warriors, their skills honed for survival in this harsh new land. They mapped the coastline, noting hidden inlets and rocky outcroppings. They studied the terrain, searching for natural formations that could conceal their precious cargo.

Their initial explorations revealed a land of breathtaking beauty, yet also of considerable danger. The forests were thick and dark, teeming with unseen creatures; the mountains were steep and unforgiving; and the weather, capricious and unpredictable, swung from brilliant sunshine to torrential rain in the space of an hour.

Brother Thomas, a scholar and cartographer by trade, meticulously documented their findings. He sketched the contours of the land, noting the location of rivers, streams, and potential trails. He was a meticulous man, his attention to detail proving invaluable as they searched for a suitable hiding place. He believed that a place naturally defended, shrouded by nature itself, would provide the best protection for the relics. A cave system, perhaps, hidden deep within a mountainside, or a secluded island inaccessible to all but the most determined explorers.

Days bled into weeks as their search continued. They encountered wildlife – majestic deer, elusive foxes, and birds of prey that circled overhead with keen, watchful eyes. They learned to navigate the treacherous terrain, their movements guided by instinct and experience. They discovered a wealth of edible plants, berries, and mushrooms, supplementing their dwindling supplies. The harshness of the land tested their resilience, yet it also forged a stronger bond between them. They were no longer just knights; they were brothers, united by a shared purpose and a common danger.

One evening, while exploring a narrow, winding river, Brother Etienne, a veteran of countless battles, stumbled upon a narrow opening in a cliff face. It was barely visible, concealed by dense foliage, a secret revealed only to the keenest of eyes. Curiosity piqued, the knights cautiously approached, their weapons at the ready. The opening led to a dark, narrow passage, the air thick with the scent of damp earth and something else... something ancient, and mysteriously enticing.

With torches flickering in the gloom, they ventured into the unknown. The passage twisted and turned, descending deeper into the earth. The air grew colder, damper, the silence broken only by the drip, drip, drip of water. After what seemed like an eternity, the passage opened into a vast cavern, its walls adorned with strange rock formations, illuminated by their flickering torches. The sheer scale of the cavern was awe-inspiring. It was a natural cathedral, a hidden sanctuary untouched by the hand of man.

Sir Geoffroi, his eyes wide with astonishment, felt a sense of profound relief. This was it, the perfect hiding place. The cavern offered unparalleled security, hidden from view, shrouded by the forest and the river. Its natural defenses, combined with the ingenuity of the Knights Templar, would create an impenetrable fortress for their sacred treasures.

The work began immediately. The knights, utilizing their combined skills, meticulously prepared the cavern. They cleared a space for the relics, creating a secure chamber within the cavern. They devised a complex system of booby traps, utilizing the natural features of the cavern to their advantage. Hidden passages, concealed openings, and pressure-sensitive mechanisms would deter any intruders, ensuring that their sacred trust remained safe.

Days turned into weeks, and weeks into months, as they worked tirelessly, their hands calloused and their bodies weary. The harsh climate tested their limits, but their

determination remained unshaken. Each knight contributed his unique skills, from carpentry and masonry to engineering and mechanics. They were architects, engineers, and guardians, all rolled into one. The task was immense, requiring meticulous planning, painstaking execution, and unwavering commitment.

Brother Thomas, true to his nature, meticulously documented every detail of their work, creating maps and diagrams of the cavern's interior. He also cataloged the relics, recording their condition and their significance. His detailed records, painstakingly crafted, would serve as a testament to their efforts, a guide for future generations who might one day inherit their sacred trust.

The work finally reached completion. The relics, carefully concealed within the cavern's secret chamber, lay protected behind layers of ingenious booby traps. The entrance to the cavern was carefully disguised, camouflaged to blend seamlessly with the surrounding landscape. The Knights Templar had found their sanctuary, a hidden fortress against the storm that raged around them. Their arduous journey, fraught with danger and uncertainty, had finally reached a turning point. Their survival was no longer a matter of escaping the enemy; now it was a matter of remaining hidden, and safeguarding their legacy for centuries to come.

The desolate beauty of Nova Scotia had become their

protector, its secrets guarding the secrets of the Order. They stood on the precipice of a new beginning, yet the shadow of the Papal Decree still loomed large, a constant reminder of the precariousness of their existence. The weight of their mission remained heavy on their hearts. They were safe, for now. But the fight for the survival of the Templar Order, and its sacred treasures, was far from over.

First Encounters

The first few weeks were a blur of activity, a frantic race against time to establish a semblance of normalcy amidst the alien landscape. The Knights, accustomed to the bustling markets and sun-drenched streets of Jerusalem, found themselves grappling with the raw, untamed beauty of the Nova Scotian wilderness. The towering pines, their branches intertwined like skeletal fingers, cast long shadows across the forest floor, a perpetual twilight that unsettled them. The silence, broken only by the whisper of the wind through the trees and the cry of unseen birds, was a profound change from the cacophony of their former lives.

Their initial forays into the surrounding woods were marked by a profound sense of unease. The land, seemingly empty, felt strangely watchful. The rustling of leaves, the snapping of a twig, sent shivers down their spines, each sound amplified by the oppressive silence. They moved with caution, their swords always at the ready, their senses heightened, expecting an ambush that never came. The very air seemed charged with an unseen energy, the palpable presence of something ancient and unknown. This was not the familiar battleground of the Crusades; this was a different kind of war, a war against the unknown, against the very elements themselves.

One crisp autumn afternoon, while Brother Thomas was foraging for berries near the edge of the forest, he stumbled upon a small clearing. A wisp of smoke curled lazily into the sky, betraying the presence of a fire. Hesitantly, he approached, his hand instinctively resting on the hilt of his sword. He saw them then, huddled around the fire – a group of Mi'kmaq people, their faces etched with a mixture of curiosity and suspicion. Their clothing, made of animal skins and woven grasses, was a stark contrast to the chainmail and tunics of the Knights Templar. They stared at him with eyes as dark and deep as the forest itself. Brother Thomas froze, unsure of how to approach them. He knew little of these people, only the whispered tales of their fierce independence and deep connection to the land.

He stood there for a long moment, caught between his

ingrained training to meet any encounter with suspicion and a growing sense of curiosity. He slowly lowered his sword, a gesture he hoped would be interpreted as peaceful. He spoke, offering a greeting in broken Latin, hoping that even a few words of shared language might bridge the cultural divide.

Their response was a low murmur, a language he did not understand, but their eyes, though still wary, seemed less hostile. One of the Mi'kmaq, an older woman with a face weathered by time and the elements, stepped forward. She offered him a piece of roasted meat, a gesture of peace, and he accepted it with a grateful bow.

The ensuing weeks saw hesitant, tentative steps towards communication. The Knights, initially wary of the

indigenous people, began to learn their ways, their customs, their language. They learned that the Mi'kmaq, though

seemingly isolated, were deeply connected to the land, living in harmony with its rhythms. They were skilled hunters and gatherers, their knowledge of the forest far exceeding that of the newcomers. The Knights, in turn, shared some of their knowledge of agriculture and metalworking, skills that proved beneficial to the Mi'kmaq. The exchange was not always easy. There were misunderstandings, moments of friction, caused by cultural differences and ingrained distrust on both sides.

One evening, while sharing stories around a crackling fire, a young Mi'kmaq warrior, named Chawke, recounted a legend of a hidden valley, a place of immense spiritual significance to his people. This valley, he claimed, held a power that could heal the sick and protect the land. He spoke of its hidden entrance, guarded by natural barriers and shrouded in mist. Brother Thomas, listening intently, noticed a striking similarity between the warrior's description and the location of the Templar's hidden chamber. The coincidence was too significant to ignore. Could the legend be linked to their hidden treasure? Could the Mi'kmaq have known about the Templar's presence all along?

The question hung heavy in the air, a palpable tension that tightened the bonds of brotherhood and community. The Knights, bound by their oath of secrecy, found themselves grappling with a moral dilemma. Should they reveal their secret to their newfound allies? The risk of exposure was enormous, the consequences potentially devastating. Yet, the possibility of forging a genuine alliance with the Mi'kmaq, a people who lived in such harmony with the land, was equally tempting. The trust had been painstakingly built, fragile as a spider's web, yet undeniably present. They found themselves caught between the demands of their sacred mission and the burgeoning sense of kinship with these people.

The days continued to unfold in a quiet rhythm of work and uneasy anticipation. The Knights helped the Mi'kmaq with their harvest, sharing their meager stores of food in return for their invaluable knowledge of the land. They learned to hunt and fish, adopting some of the indigenous techniques that proved more efficient and sustainable than their own. The language barrier remained a significant challenge, but through gestures, shared experiences, and a mutual respect for survival, they found a way to communicate. The old woman, who had first offered Brother Thomas the meat, became a vital link between the two cultures, translating stories and bridging the gap between their vastly different worlds.

Slowly, cautiously, trust began to blossom. The initial

suspicion gave way to cautious curiosity, and eventually to a fragile, tentative friendship. The Knights Templar,

accustomed to the rigid hierarchies of their order, found themselves adapting to a more egalitarian society. They learned to appreciate the Mi'kmaq's deep respect for the land and their reverence for nature. The Mi'kmaq, in turn, were fascinated by the Knights' tales of faraway lands and their unwavering faith. The common ground they found in their shared struggle for survival and the desire to protect their homes forged an unlikely bond. Their shared humanity transcended the vast chasm of language and culture, proving that some things, such as friendship and survival, are

universal.

But the shadow of the Papal Decree still loomed large, a constant reminder of their precarious existence. The hidden chamber remained their most precious secret, a burden they carried with them into their new life. The knowledge of the Mi'kmaq's legend, and the eerie similarities to their own hidden sanctuary, added another layer of complexity to their already fraught situation. Their new-found friendship was a blessing and a potential curse, for it came at a time when the weight of their secret threatened to overwhelm them. Their survival, once a matter of escaping the clutches of their enemies, now included the delicate task of preserving the trust they had so carefully cultivated with their new allies. The future remained uncertain, filled with both hope and a deep, persistent fear that their carefully constructed world could crumble at any moment. The journey had taken them from the heart of Christendom to the edge of the known world. The Knights Templar were far from home, but at least, for now, they had found a haven, a fragile peace, in this remote corner of the earth.

Choosing the Site

The salt spray stung their faces as the battered longship finally grounded on the rocky Nova Scotian shore. The journey from Jerusalem had been arduous, a relentless test of endurance against the unforgiving sea. The escape itself, a desperate dash through the increasingly hostile streets of the Holy City, felt like a lifetime ago. Now, the weight of their mission pressed down on the remaining Knights Templar –the safeguarding of the sacred relics entrusted to their care.

Their future, their very survival, depended on choosing wisely. Finding a sanctuary in this untamed land was their immediate, paramount concern.

Brother Thomas, his weathered face etched with lines of worry and determination, studied the coastline. The wind howled, whipping his grey hair across his eyes. He was their leader now, the weight of command heavy on his shoulders. He'd seen many battles, but this, this was a different kind of war – a fight for survival against the very fabric of their existence, outlawed and hunted by the very Church they had sworn to defend. He ran a hand through his thinning beard, the salt clinging to the rough strands.

"We need to be discreet," he said, his voice barely audible above the roar of the wind. "Our enemies will be looking for us. They will stop at nothing to reclaim what they believe is rightfully theirs."

Sir Geoffry, his youthful face still bearing the marks of recent battles, nodded grimly. He was one of the youngest, his enthusiasm tempered by the harsh reality of their situation. He had witnessed firsthand the brutality of the French Inquisition, the fiery deaths of his brothers-in-arms.

The memory fueled his determination. "We need a place impregnable, Brother Thomas. A place they'll never find."

The other surviving knights, a band of seasoned warriors, concurred. Their numbers were fewer than they had hoped, many having succumbed to disease, exhaustion, or the violence inflicted upon them along the way. Yet, their commitment remained unshaken. The sacred relics – the fragments of the True Cross, the chalice rumored to be used at the Last Supper, and other precious artifacts – represented more than just religious significance. They were symbols of faith, hope, and the enduring legacy of the Knights Templar.

The search began. Days bled into weeks, marked only by the rhythmic crashing of waves against the shore and the

endless, unforgiving expanse of the wilderness. The knights explored, inching their way into the dense forests, crossing treacherous rivers, and climbing rugged mountains. Their knowledge of the land was limited, their reliance on the sparse maps they had managed to salvage meager.

The criteria were stringent. The chosen site had to be

naturally concealed, offering protection from the elements and, critically, from unwanted visitors. Proximity to a water source was essential, as was some form of defensible terrain– natural barriers that would hinder potential attackers. Above all, secrecy was paramount.

They considered several locations. One promising site was a cave system near the coast, its entrance hidden behind a cascading waterfall, a natural veil against prying eyes.

However, access to the interior was difficult and the cave itself felt too exposed. Another location, nestled deep within a dense forest, offered natural camouflage, but lacked a readily available water source.

Then, Brother Etienne, a man whose quiet demeanor concealed a keen eye for detail, pointed towards a remote, rocky peninsula jutting out into the ocean. It was a place of stark beauty, windswept and formidable. At its heart lay a deep, almost hidden fissure in the cliffs. The entrance was obscured by dense vegetation and boulders, appearing to be nothing more than a natural rock formation.

"This," Brother Etienne stated, his voice low, "is the place."

As they explored the fissure, they discovered a large, cavernous space within the cliff face. It was dry, spacious, and offered ample room to build a vault. The entrance could be expertly concealed, rendered almost invisible to casual observation. Moreover, the peninsula's isolated location and the challenging terrain surrounding it provided a formidable natural defense.

The decision was unanimous. This was their sanctuary, their refuge from the storm.

The construction of the vault began immediately. They worked with feverish intensity, fueled by a mixture of fear, determination, and a deep sense of religious conviction.

They used the rudimentary tools they had salvaged, their hands roughened and bleeding from the labor. They dug, they hauled stones, and they fashioned timbers into a sturdy framework.

The vault itself was built of hand-hewn stones, layered with meticulous care. They reinforced the structure with wooden beams and covered the exterior with a layer of earth and vegetation, effectively camouflaging it within the cliff face. But their preparations extended beyond mere construction.

The Knights Templar were masters of military engineering, and they applied their expertise to designing a sophisticated system of booby traps to protect their treasure. Pressure plates concealed within the ground triggered hidden pitfalls and sharpened stakes. Tripwires connected to concealed caltrops lay in wait for any intruders who managed to bypass the initial defenses. They even incorporated a system of hidden passages and secret chambers to further confound any potential attackers.

The process of placing the relics within the vault was a solemn affair. Each artifact was carefully wrapped in layers of protective cloth, then enshrined in individual wooden cases. Brother Thomas led the knights in prayers and rituals, their voices echoing through the cavernous space. It was a sacred act, a profound acknowledgment of the responsibility entrusted to them.

Once the relics were securely placed within the heart of the vault, the entrance was sealed. The surrounding area was meticulously cleared of any debris that might reveal their presence. They used native plants and natural materials to blend the entrance seamlessly with the surrounding cliff face, making it look as if it were a part of the natural landscape.

Finally, a camouflage of skillfully arranged vegetation obscured the entrance completely, rendering it virtually invisible to the untrained eye. The entrance was not just hidden, it was cleverly disguised, a testament to the Templar's ingenuity and dedication to preserving their sacred legacy. Their work was complete. For now, at least, they were safe. Their sanctuary was established. The perilous journey was far from over, but they had found a foothold in the untamed wilderness – a place to gather strength, to regroup, and to prepare for what lay ahead. The relentless pursuit of their enemies was a certainty, but within the heart of their newly constructed sanctuary, a flicker of hope remained, shielded from the encroaching darkness.

Construction of the Vault

The initial task was to locate a suitable site. Days were spent traversing the unforgiving terrain, their eyes scanning the landscape for a place that offered both concealment and natural defenses. Finally, they settled upon a secluded cove, nestled deep within a dense forest, where a rocky outcrop offered the perfect foundation for their subterranean sanctuary. The very geography itself seemed to conspire with their need for secrecy. The cove was almost inaccessible from the land, guarded by treacherous cliffs and tangled undergrowth. Only the sea offered a reasonable approach, and even then, the rocky shoreline would present a

formidable challenge to any uninvited guests.

The construction was a monumental undertaking, a

testament to the Knights' unwavering dedication and their mastery of engineering. They worked tirelessly, driven by a sense of urgency that gnawed at their souls. Each man possessed skills honed over years of service, skills now put to a desperate, almost desperate use. Sir Geoffrey, the most experienced among them in matters of fortification, oversaw the entire operation, his knowledge of ancient building techniques proving invaluable. He had served in many sieges, witnessed the construction and destruction of countless strongholds, and had learned to appreciate the importance of both solidity and cunning design.

The first step involved excavating the vault itself. Using simple tools fashioned from salvaged materials and

sharpened stones, they painstakingly carved into the rock, their progress slow but steady. The earth was hard, resisting their efforts with stubborn determination. Sweat beaded on their brows, and exhaustion settled upon their weary limbs.

Yet, they persevered, fueled by the sacred responsibility they bore and the knowledge that the fate of their order, indeed the future of their faith, might rest upon their shoulders.

The dimensions of the vault were carefully planned, large enough to accommodate the precious relics yet compact enough to remain hidden. A network of tunnels, strategically placed and meticulously camouflaged, would serve as an escape route, adding an extra layer of security to their hidden haven. The walls were reinforced with layers of stone, bound together with a mortar mixture painstakingly crafted from local materials. Each stone was placed with precision, ensuring both structural integrity and a seamless, almost invisible blending into the surrounding rock.

The entrance to the vault was the most crucial aspect of the entire project. It needed to be both secure and virtually undetectable. They chose a spot shielded by a dense thicket of trees, their branches hanging low to obscure the view. The opening itself was cunningly disguised as a natural rock formation. Sir Aymeric, a master of camouflage and deception, was instrumental in this stage of the construction.

He oversaw the careful placement of rocks and vegetation, mimicking the surrounding landscape perfectly. The entrance was not just hidden, it was effectively erased from view.

But mere concealment wasn't enough. The Templars knew that their enemies were tenacious and resourceful. Therefore, they integrated a series of booby traps into the design. These were not mere obstacles; they were sophisticated mechanisms designed to inflict serious damage, or even death, upon any intruders.

The first line of defense was a system of pressure plates cleverly concealed beneath the concealing vegetation.

Stepping on these plates would trigger a cascade of sharpened stakes, concealed in the surrounding undergrowth, to spring upwards with deadly force. These were not flimsy mechanisms. Each stake was meticulously sharpened and reinforced, guaranteed to pierce armor and flesh alike. The placement of these plates was cunning, designed to force any intruder into a predetermined path, making escape impossible.

Beyond the pressure plates, a maze-like series of tunnels added further complexity. These tunnels were narrow, dark, and designed to disorient any intruders, making their progress slow and unpredictable. At strategic points along these tunnels, hidden pits waited, camouflaged to appear as solid ground. Any unwary trespasser would plummet into the depths, potentially breaking limbs or suffering worse. The bottom of each pit was lined with sharpened rocks, further increasing the risk of severe injury.

Near the vault entrance itself, a more sophisticated booby trap was installed. This was a system of tripwires, intricately woven into the surrounding vegetation. These wires were almost invisible, yet incredibly strong, capable of triggering a massive boulder to roll from the cliff above. The sheer weight and momentum of the boulder would ensure that any intruder who triggered this trap would be crushed without mercy. The precision and deadly efficacy of this trap showed the Knights' understanding of mechanics and their unwavering dedication to securing their sacred legacy.

Finally, at the very entrance to the vault itself, a final layer of defense was implemented. This was a complex system of levers and counterweights, designed to seal the entrance instantly upon the triggering of any of the previously mentioned traps. The speed and effectiveness of the mechanism would render any attempts at forced entry futile, effectively trapping any intruders in their own deadly game.

The heavy stone slab sealing the entrance would be held in place by an intricate system of locks, all secured with keys only the Knights possessed.

The construction of the vault was a collaborative effort, each Knight contributing their specific skills and knowledge.

Their tireless work, fueled by both faith and fear,

transformed a rugged cove into an impenetrable fortress. It was a testament to their resilience and ingenuity, a testament to their determination to protect the sacred relics entrusted to their care. The seemingly endless hours of hard labor were punctuated by moments of quiet contemplation, their hearts heavy with the weight of their mission. They had successfully established a sanctuary, a bastion against the encroaching darkness, a secure vault for their sacred heritage. But their ordeal was far from over. The relentless pursuit of their enemies would continue, and the shadows of the past would continue to stretch towards them, testing their brotherhood to the very limit. The vault was a haven, but it was also a promise – a promise to protect and preserve, to endure, and to ultimately triumph over the forces that sought to erase them. The construction was complete, a monument to the enduring spirit of the Knights Templar.

Concealing the Entrance

The final touches were painstaking, demanding an almost obsessive attention to detail. Sir Geoffroi, a master

stonemason before his Templar vows, oversaw the

meticulous blending of the vault's entrance with the natural rock face. He and his brethren spent days chipping away at the surrounding stone, carefully shaping and texturing the newly laid blocks to mirror the weathered appearance of the cliff face. They employed a technique passed down through generations of Templar builders – a subtle interplay of light and shadow, achieved through precise placement of stones and the careful application of lichen and moss collected from the deeper recesses of the forest. From a distance, the

entrance was entirely invisible, a seamless continuation of the rock itself.

Beyond mere visual deception, they incorporated a more intricate system of misdirection. A winding, seemingly natural fissure in the cliff face, a feature easily overlooked amidst the rugged terrain, was cleverly incorporated into the entrance's design. This fissure, a deceptive dead end, served as a perfect decoy, drawing the eyes of any potential intruder away from the true entrance which was skillfully concealed behind a carefully positioned boulder, appearing merely as another element of the chaotic natural landscape.

The boulder itself was no ordinary rock. Chosen for its size and weight, it was a formidable barrier, but its placement was the key. It rested precariously, seemingly held in place only by gravity and the natural irregularities of the surrounding rock. Its seemingly unstable position was, however, a carefully calculated deception. A complex system of levers and counterweights, concealed beneath the mossy earth, allowed the boulder to be moved, revealing the vault's true entrance only when triggered by a precise sequence of actions, known only to the remaining Templars.

To further enhance security, they utilized a system of

concealed tripwires, leading away from the main approach. Thin, almost invisible strands of strong, tanned leather were expertly woven into the undergrowth, virtually undetectable amidst the dense vegetation. Should an intruder inadvertently trip these wires, a series of booby traps would be activated, ranging from the relatively harmless – a cascade of rocks and debris – to the potentially lethal –sharpened stakes concealed within the soil. These traps were designed not to kill, but to deter and delay, providing the Knights with valuable time to react. The primary objective was not to inflict harm but to buy them time, allowing them to escape or prepare for defense.

Their ingenuity extended to the very air itself. The Templars, understanding the power of sound and echo, cleverly manipulated the acoustics of the cove. The surrounding terrain was carefully analyzed, and specific features were used to subtly alter the soundscape, masking any sounds emanating from the vault's interior. This meant that any sounds produced within would seem to originate from somewhere else entirely, further concealing the location of the entrance. The entrance was effectively silenced, hidden not just visually but aurally. The very wind whistling

through the crags seemed to conspire in their deception.

The final, and perhaps most ingenious, element of

concealment was the use of natural camouflage. Once the entrance was sealed, the Templars meticulously covered the area with earth, meticulously replicating the surrounding soil and vegetation. They carefully selected plants and moss, ensuring that the camouflage was seamless and indistinguishable from its surroundings. This wasn't a hasty, rough job; it was a work of art, designed to blend the entrance perfectly with the landscape. Over time, nature would do the rest. Seeds of local flora were carefully sown, encouraging natural growth and further obscuring the work of their hands.

The entire process was a testament to the Knights' resourcefulness and determination. Their skills, honed through years of military training and devout religious practice, were combined with the knowledge and instinct of those who lived close to the land. Their understanding of the natural world was crucial to their success. Every element of concealment, from the strategic placement of stones to the subtle manipulation of acoustics, reflected their keen observation and deep understanding of the environment.

This sanctuary, their final refuge, was not just a physical structure but a testament to the enduring spirit and cunning intellect of the Knights Templar.

The days bled into weeks, the weeks into months, as the Knights tirelessly worked, their dedication unwavering. Each man played a vital role, their collective skills complementing each other. Sir Jean, a scholar and cartographer, meticulously charted the area, ensuring the precise placement of each trap and counterweight. Sir Guillaume, skilled in the art of herbalism, identified the most effective plants for camouflage, carefully ensuring they would thrive in the harsh Nova Scotian climate. And even Brother Thomas, the youngest and seemingly least experienced, proved invaluable, possessing an innate understanding of the local wildlife and their patterns, knowledge vital in predicting potential disruptions to their elaborate camouflage.

As the entrance became increasingly indistinguishable from its surroundings, the Knights took time to reflect upon their

Monumental undertaking. They stood before their sanctuary, a feeling of immense pride and relief mixed with the profound solemnity of their perilous task. This wasn't simply a hiding place; it was a testament to their faith, a symbol of their unwavering commitment to preserving their sacred legacy despite the overwhelming odds against them. The weight of their history, the burden of their secret, had been transferred from their shoulders to the silent strength of the earth. The sanctuary wasn't merely a refuge from the world; it was a physical embodiment of their resilience, their faith, and their unshakeable hope in the face of adversity.

The work, however, was not yet complete. The vault itself required further preparation. Within its depths lay the precious relics, artifacts of immense religious and historical significance. The protection of these holy objects demanded even greater care and secrecy. The internal structure of the vault, its internal mechanisms, and the preservation of its contents required equal attention and ingenuity. They had successfully concealed the entrance, but the real work, the true preservation of their legacy, lay ahead. The task of securing the relics and ensuring their survival through the ages was just beginning. The successful concealment of the entrance was a significant milestone, a testament to their skill and determination, but it was merely the first step in a far greater, far more complex endeavor. The Knights knew this, and their weariness did not overshadow their commitment to the sacred duty that still remained.

The setting sun cast long shadows across the rugged

landscape, painting the cove in hues of orange and purple. As darkness fell, the Knights gathered around a small fire, the flickering flames dancing in their eyes. They shared a silent meal, their minds filled with a mixture of relief and apprehension. Their sanctuary was complete, at least as far as the entrance was concerned. The earth itself had become their confidante, the stones their silent allies. But the path ahead remained fraught with uncertainty, and the specter of their pursuers still loomed large. They would continue their vigilance, aware that their work was far from over, and their struggle to protect their heritage would likely continue for many years to come, perhaps even generations. The sanctuary was built, the entrance concealed, but the true test of their faith and resilience was yet to come. Their journey had reached a critical juncture. They had built their refuge, now they would need to safeguard the secret within,

ensuring its survival against all odds. The future was

uncertain, but one thing was clear: the Knights Templar would never surrender. Their commitment to their faith, their brotherhood, and their sacred mission remained unbreakable. The sanctuary stood as a testament to their enduring spirit, a silent promise whispered across the rugged landscape of Nova Scotia.

Securing the Relics

The air hung heavy with the scent of pine and damp earth, a stark contrast to the incense that Brother Thomas, their chaplain, was meticulously preparing. He moved with the quiet grace of a seasoned ritualist, his movements precise and deliberate as he arranged the silver censers and prepared the consecrated bread and wine. The vault, hewn from the solid rock, felt both ancient and new, a space born of necessity and faith. Its rough-hewn walls seemed to breathe, a silent testament to the arduous labor of the past weeks. Torches flickered, casting dancing shadows that seemed to writhe and twist like ancient spirits.

Sir Geoffroi, his face etched with the weariness of their long journey and relentless toil, checked the final security

measures. The entrance, flawlessly integrated with the cliff face, was sealed by a massive stone, its weight reinforced by a system of hidden levers and counterweights, a masterpiece of engineering and deception. He ran a calloused hand over the cold, smooth surface, a silent prayer passing his lips.

The relics, carefully wrapped in layers of soft linen and secured in oak chests, were brought forth. Each chest bore the weight of centuries, their surfaces worn smooth with time and bearing the scars of countless journeys across continents. There was the chalice, rumored to have been used by Christ at the Last Supper, its silver dulled but its aura undeniable. Then, the fragment of the True Cross, a small piece of wood, yet radiating an almost palpable sanctity. And lastly, the seemingly simple cloth, believed to be a piece of the Virgin Mary's veil, its delicate weave still miraculously intact despite its age. Each relic was handled with the utmost reverence, each knight pausing to offer a silent prayer.

The ritual began. Brother Thomas, his voice resonating with deep faith, chanted ancient Latin prayers, the words echoing in the cavernous space. The flickering torchlight illuminated the solemn faces of the knights, their armor glinting in the unsteady light. They formed a circle around the chests, their faces etched with devotion, their posture reflecting their years of military discipline. Each knight, in turn, touched the chests, offering a wordless blessing, a silent pledge to protect the sacred contents entrusted to their care.

Sir Aymeric, the leader of the remaining Templars, stepped forward. His face, usually stoic and hardened by years of battle, held a poignant mixture of grief and determination. He spoke in a low voice, his words barely audible above the crackling of the torches, but full of an unwavering conviction. "Brothers," he began, "we stand here at the precipice of a new era. An era where our order, unjustly condemned, must find a new path, a new sanctuary. Our sacred mission continues, though its form is transformed. We are the keepers of a legacy, the custodians of faith itself. Let these relics, symbols of our unwavering belief, be a testament to our enduring spirit."

A profound silence followed his words. Each man felt the weight of history pressing down on them, the burden of protecting their faith against a tide of persecution. The

silence was then broken only by Brother Thomas's continued chanting, a counterpoint to the deep emotions that filled the vault. As he concluded the prayers, a palpable sense of peace settled over the assembled knights. They were not simply hiding relics; they were safeguarding the very heart of their faith. They were preserving a legacy for future generations, a beacon of hope in a world consumed by darkness.

The process of placing the relics into their designated niches was slow and deliberate. Each chest was carefully lowered into its place, secured with hidden mechanisms that would make their retrieval nearly impossible. Sir Geoffroi, with the assistance of others, meticulously tested the locking mechanisms, ensuring that the relics would remain safely concealed. The precision and skill demonstrated by these warriors was remarkable. It was not merely the brute force of soldiers but the deft hands of artisans, the ingenuity of master craftsmen. The construction was as much a work of art as a defensive fortress.

As the final chest was secured, a wave of exhaustion washed over the knights. They had persevered through unimaginable hardships, fleeing persecution, enduring a perilous journey across the ocean, and toiling tirelessly to construct this sanctuary. Yet, in this moment of completion, they were infused with a profound sense of satisfaction, their faith renewed by the sacred task they had undertaken. The vault held more than just religious artifacts; it contained the indomitable spirit of an order that had been unjustly condemned, a testament to their unshakeable resolve, a beacon of hope for a future that was still uncertain.

The work, however, was far from over. Sir Aymeric reminded them that the physical security of the vault was only one aspect of their mission. The true test lay in safeguarding their secret from the outside world. The entrance might be concealed, but the knowledge of its existence, the very knowledge of their survival, remained a potentially fatal vulnerability. A network of spies, false trails, and coded messages would need to be established to ensure their survival, to safeguard the sanctuary and its precious contents from those who would seek to destroy it, either for religious or political gain.

He outlined a plan for a system of rotating guards, each Templar responsible for a specific period of watch. Regular patrols of the surrounding area would be necessary to detect any potential intruders, and an intricate network of signals would be established to communicate between the sanctuary and their few remaining allies scattered across the countryside. Secrecy was their most potent weapon, and vigilance their most unwavering ally. Their lives, and their sacred mission, depended on it.

The next few days were spent preparing for this new phase of their mission. They meticulously mapped out patrol routes, planned a system of coded messages using rocks, trees, and other natural features of the landscape, and established a set of contingencies for various scenarios, from surprise attacks to natural disasters. They established a strict code of silence, even amongst themselves, each Templar pledging absolute discretion in protecting their secret. There were moments of quiet reflection, moments where the weight of their responsibility pressed down on them. Yet, amidst the tension, a renewed sense of purpose bound them together, a shared commitment to safeguarding their heritage, their faith, and their future. Their task was monumental, yet their determination unyielding.

The sanctuary, a fortress carved from the very heart of the earth, stood as a silent sentinel, a testament to their courage, their faith, and their unwavering resolve. The relics within were not merely objects of religious significance; they were symbols of hope, emblems of resilience in the face of adversity, and a legacy of faith for generations to come.

Their task was never truly finished, always vigilance and care was required, always there was a new enemy to face. But for now, in the quiet solitude of their secluded sanctuary, the last of the Templars had found a respite, a place where they could begin to rebuild their world, one stone, one prayer, one act of faith at a time. The future remained uncertain, filled with potential dangers, but the knights faced it together, bound by their sacred mission, their unwavering faith, and their enduring brotherhood. The relics were secure, for now. But the fight to protect their legacy was far from over.

The First Defense

The rhythmic clang of hammer against steel echoed through the cavernous space, a counterpoint to the hushed whispers of the knights. Sir Geoffrey, his face grim but determined, oversaw the construction of the outer defenses. He'd spent years in the Holy Land, facing down Saladin's forces, and the subtle art of fortification was ingrained in his very bones.

This wasn't just a sanctuary; it was a last stand, a bastion against a world that had turned against them. The rough-hewn stones, painstakingly hauled from the nearby quarry, were being shaped and fitted with a precision born of desperation and unwavering resolve.

Each stone was a prayer, each carefully placed timber a testament to their enduring faith. The knights, their faces streaked with sweat and grime, worked with a feverish energy, fueled by a shared sense of purpose. They were not merely building a wall; they were building a shield, a bulwark against the storm that raged beyond the mountain's embrace. Their hammers rang out a defiant anthem against the encroaching darkness, a promise that their legacy would not be easily extinguished.

Beyond the immediate vicinity of the sanctuary's entrance, a network of concealed pits and trenches were being dug. These were not mere obstacles; they were carefully designed death traps, the legacy of years spent battling across the Holy Land. Sir Aymeric, a seasoned veteran of countless sieges, meticulously oversaw the construction of these deadly impediments. Each pit was strategically placed, camouflaged with earth and brush, designed to ensnare and disable any unsuspecting intruders. Spiked wooden stakes, sharpened to lethal points, were concealed beneath the surface, poised to impale anyone foolish enough to stumble into their path. The knights worked silently, their movements precise and efficient, each knowing the value of their efforts.

The air hung thick with the scent of pine, damp earth, and the metallic tang of blood, a grim reminder of the battles they had fought and those yet to come. The flickering

torchlight danced on their faces, illuminating the grim

determination etched into their features. Brother Thomas, his face pale but resolute, moved amongst them, offering words of comfort and encouragement. He was their spiritual guide, their anchor in the storm, and his presence brought a measure of solace to their weary hearts. He quietly muttered prayers for their safety and for the success of their mission, his voice a low hum amidst the din of construction.

As the sun began its descent, casting long shadows across the rugged landscape, the outer perimeter began to take shape. A high wall of rough-hewn stone, reinforced with sturdy timbers, encircled the sanctuary's entrance. The wall was not uniformly constructed; irregular gaps and

protrusions had been deliberately left in place to serve as firing positions and observation points. These irregular

features served a double purpose: providing natural cover for the knights defending the perimeter and making any approach by an enemy more difficult to plan and manage.

Beyond the wall, a network of carefully concealed obstacles stretched outward, a silent testament to the Templars' ingenuity and determination. Hidden pits, treacherous

trenches, and cleverly placed stakes formed a deadly

labyrinth, designed to slow, disorient, and ultimately defeat any potential attackers. This intricate system of defenses was not just a barrier; it was a carefully orchestrated dance of death, conceived and executed by the most skilled warriors of their time.

The knights continued working until long after darkness had fallen, illuminated only by the flickering torches that cast dancing shadows across their grim faces. They worked silently, driven by a profound sense of purpose. Theirs was not a task of simple defense; it was a sacred mission, a testament to their unwavering faith and unshakeable resolve. They were defending not just a place; they were defending their legacy, the legacy of the Knights Templar, a legacy that had been unjustly extinguished, but which they were

determined to preserve.

Once darkness fully consumed the area, the knights

established lookouts on the highest points, where they could survey the area. The use of flares or smoke signals would help signal any approaching threat. The terrain was rugged, providing natural barriers, but that very roughness made it dangerous as well. They established a system of patrols to cover the perimeter. Each patrol was composed of two knights, each armed with swords, axes, and lances. They moved quietly, their steps muffled by the soft earth, their senses alert, their eyes scanning the darkness for any sign of movement.

The cold night air bit at their exposed skin, but the knights bore the discomfort without complaint. Their dedication to their mission outweighed their discomfort. They understood the gravity of their situation. They were the last of their kind, the remnants of a proud order, unjustly accused and relentlessly pursued. Their sanctuary was more than a physical space; it was a refuge, a symbol of their enduring faith and resilience. And they were prepared to defend it to the death. Their faith was their armor, and their brotherhood their shield.

Inside the sanctuary, Brother Thomas conducted a solemn prayer service. The knights knelt in silent prayer, their faces illuminated by the soft glow of the candles. They prayed for strength, for guidance, for protection. They were not just defending a physical space; they were defending their faith, their history, their very identity. The weight of this responsibility rested heavily upon their shoulders. Each knight felt it. Each was ready to shoulder this weight.

The days that followed were a blur of activity. The knights continued to refine their defenses, adding layers of protection that seemed almost impossible to penetrate. They constructed additional barricades, strengthened weak points, and created new traps, constantly adapting to the challenges posed by their harsh environment. The surrounding landscape became their ally, forming a treacherous maze for anyone who might attempt to breach their defenses.

They also began stockpiling supplies. They gathered firewood, hunted for game, and collected water. They established a system of rationing, ensuring that their supplies would last as long as possible. Brother Thomas, ever the pragmatist, ensured that spiritual sustenance was not neglected. Daily prayers, communal meals, and mutual support helped maintain the spirits of the men, keeping them united. The fear was there, yet they fought to maintain unity, their shared purpose.

Sir Geoffrey and Sir Aymeric, always vigilant, spent hours studying the terrain, identifying potential vulnerabilities and developing strategies to counter any potential threats. They were skilled strategists, honed by years of experience in warfare, and their knowledge proved invaluable in bolstering their defense. They knew that their sanctuary was not impregnable; it could be breached, given sufficient effort and determination. But they also knew that they would make any such attempt costly and bloody. Their defenses were designed not just to prevent attack, but also to inflict maximum damage upon any intruders.

As the weeks turned into months, the sanctuary became a self-sufficient fortress, a microcosm of a world that had turned its back on them. They learned to live in harmony with their surroundings, drawing strength from the harsh yet rewarding wilderness. The land provided for them, and they, in turn, showed respect for the sacred ground.

Yet, even as they strengthened their defenses, they knew that their vigilance could not falter. The threat remained. The world that once held them in high esteem was now

determined to erase them. They were outlaws, hunted men, but their spirits were unbroken. They had found refuge in this isolated sanctuary, but their struggle was far from over. The fight for their legacy, for their faith, and for their very survival was only just beginning. The silence of their isolated sanctuary only served to heighten their awareness, making them keenly attuned to the slightest sound or movement. The sanctuary was their refuge, but also their battleground. Their survival depended not just on their weapons and defenses, but on their unity, their faith, and their unyielding resolve.

Adapting to the New Land

The biting wind whipped across the barren landscape, a stark contrast to the sun-drenched hills of Jerusalem. Sir Geoffroi, his breath misting in the frigid air, shivered despite the thick wool cloak draped over his shoulders. Nova Scotia, their new haven, was a land of unforgiving beauty. The towering pines, skeletal against the grey sky, offered little shelter from the relentless wind that howled through the valleys, a constant reminder of their exile. The lush, fertile lands they had envisioned from the fragmented maps were proving to be far more challenging. The soil, unforgiving and rocky, offered little in the way of easy cultivation. The forests, while vast, were dense and difficult to navigate, their depths concealing both sustenance and peril. Their initial attempts at foraging had yielded meager results; the unfamiliar plants and berries were a gamble, and several brothers had suffered from painful digestive upsets.

The initial shock of their arrival had given way to a grim determination. They were Knights Templar, after all, trained for hardship and adversity. The discipline forged in years of warfare and religious devotion would not desert them now.

Brother Thomas, ever practical, had taken the lead in establishing a rudimentary shelter. Using felled timber and branches scavenged from the forest, he had constructed a series of lean-tos, providing a modicum of protection from the elements. The crude structures were far from comfortable, but they were better than exposure to the unrelenting elements.

Their survival hinged on their ability to adapt. Their knowledge of siege warfare and defensive tactics was of little use in this new struggle for existence. They were no longer warriors defending Christendom; they were pioneers wrestling with the harsh realities of a wild and unfamiliar land. Hunting became a daily necessity. Sir Geoffroi, along with several others, honed their hunting skills, adapting their techniques to the local wildlife. Deer, initially elusive, eventually became a source of meat, although procuring them demanded patience, stealth, and often, a fierce struggle.

Trapping, a skill some of the brothers possessed, proved invaluable, supplementing their meager hunting successes with rabbits and smaller game.

The challenges extended beyond mere sustenance. Clothing, worn thin from their arduous journey, offered little protection against the cold. Brother Etienne, a master craftsman back in Jerusalem, demonstrated remarkable ingenuity, using animal hides and woven plant fibers to create makeshift garments and blankets. Their boots, originally intended for the dusty roads of the Holy Land, were failing to provide adequate protection against the rough terrain and the constant dampness. Brother Jean-Luc, resourceful and observant, learned from the local indigenous people—their tentative allies—techniques for waterproofing leather and fashioning sturdy footwear.

The relentless winter tested their resolve. The snow fell heavily, blanketing the land in a thick, unforgiving layer of white. The wind howled with increasing ferocity, threatening to tear apart their fragile shelters. The long nights were filled with the eerie sounds of the wilderness, a stark reminder of their vulnerability. Food became scarce, and hunger gnawed at their bodies. Several brothers succumbed to sickness, their weakened systems unable to withstand the harsh conditions.

Brother Guillaume, a skilled herbalist, worked tirelessly, concocting remedies from the limited plant life, sometimes with questionable success. His knowledge, gleaned from ancient texts and learned during his travels in the Orient, proved invaluable to the community, yet it was a constant struggle against disease.

Despite the difficulties, the spirit of the Templars remained unbroken. Their faith, once a source of comfort in the face of persecution, became their anchor in this new, harsh reality. Daily prayers were held, their voices echoing in the desolate landscape, a testament to their unwavering devotion. The rituals provided solace and a sense of continuity, a link to the life they had left behind in the Holy Land. The shared hardships forged a stronger bond among the brothers, strengthening their resolve and fostering a deep sense of brotherhood that had survived the persecution they had endured and the arduous escape across the ocean.

The indigenous population, initially wary of these foreign newcomers, gradually came to see them as neither threat nor enemy. Their skill in hunting and trapping, along with their willingness to share their limited resources, earned them a grudging respect. Slowly, cautiously, a bond of mutual respect and sometimes even trust, began to develop. They learned from the indigenous people how to survive better in this land. They learned the local languages, the medicinal properties of the wild plants, and the ways to navigate the unforgiving terrain.

There were moments of despair, of course. The weight of their past, the memory of their brethren lost to the

Inquisition, hung heavy upon their hearts. The uncertainty of their future, their constant awareness of the possible pursuit by their enemies, cast a long shadow over their daily existence. Yet, amidst the hardships, moments of quiet beauty emerged. The breathtaking sunsets, the haunting calls of the birds, the sheer immensity of the forest – these provided moments of solace, a reminder of the beauty that still existed in the world, despite the darkness that had engulfed them.

The Templars learned that adaptation wasn't just a matter of survival, but also about transformation. They adapted their military skills to hunting, their organizational talents to building a community. Their prayers became woven into the rhythm of their daily lives, a source of strength in the face of adversity. Their shared faith, their steadfast brotherhood, their resilience and ingenuity—these qualities were not relics of the past, but tools for forging a new future in this unforgiving land. They were not merely surviving; they were evolving, becoming something new, yet retaining their core identity. They were the Knights Templar, and even in this new wilderness, their legacy would endure. The seeds of their future were sown in the harsh Nova Scotian soil, a testament to their enduring faith, their indomitable spirit, and their remarkable ability to adapt. Their ordeal was far from over, but they were ready; tempered by hardship, forged in adversity, and united by their unwavering faith.

Building a Community

The first winter was a brutal teacher. Many of the brothers, accustomed to the relatively mild climate of the Holy Land, succumbed to illness or succumbed to the unforgiving cold.

The initial shelters, hastily constructed from branches and mud, offered little protection against the relentless wind and snow. Brother Thomas, a skilled mason from Auvergne, took the lead in constructing more substantial dwellings. Using the knowledge they had gleaned from observing the indigenous Mi'kmaq, they began to build sturdy longhouses, utilizing timber frames, woven wattle and daub walls, and thatched roofs. The process was slow and laborious, each log painstakingly cut and hauled, each thatch carefully laid. But the resulting structures were a testament to their perseverance, offering warmth, relative dryness, and a sense of security.

Food remained a constant challenge. Their initial hunting efforts were clumsy and unproductive; the abundance of game they had envisioned proved elusive. Brother Etienne, a seasoned hunter from Burgundy, took the brothers under his wing, patiently teaching them the intricacies of tracking and trapping. He revealed the secrets of the forest, identifying edible plants and instructing them on methods of preserving food for the lean months ahead. They learned to snare rabbits and hunt deer, but the meat was often meager, barely enough to sustain the depleted number of surviving brothers.

Fishing, initially frustrating due to the unfamiliar waters and lack of suitable equipment, slowly became a reliable source of sustenance. Brother Guillaume, a former shipwright from Marseilles, fashioned crude fishing nets and spears, and taught the brothers the art of patiently waiting for the right moment to strike.

The organization of their community mirrored the strict hierarchy of the Templar Order, adapted to their new

circumstances. Sir Geoffroi, Grand Master of this remnant band, maintained overall leadership, delegating responsibilities based on the brothers' skills and experience.

Brother Thomas oversaw construction and maintenance, Brother Etienne managed hunting and foraging, and Brother Guillaume directed fishing and boat-building. But this was not merely a division of labor; it was a testament to the Templar spirit of unity and shared purpose. The brothers prayed together, shared their meager rations, and offered mutual support. Their faith, once a source of comfort in the Holy Land, became even more central to their lives in this harsh wilderness. Their daily prayers, punctuated by the howling wind and the creak of the longhouses, were not simply rituals; they were affirmations of their survival, testaments to their enduring hope.

The land itself presented a constant challenge. The soil, poor and rocky, stubbornly resisted their efforts at cultivation.

Their first attempts at planting yielded a meager harvest, barely enough to supplement their hunting and fishing.

Brother Jean, a former farmer from the Champagne region of France, patiently experimented with various techniques, slowly learning the nuances of the Nova Scotian soil. He experimented with different crops, adapting his methods to the unpredictable weather. His perseverance eventually brought some success: they managed to cultivate hardy vegetables, such as turnips and cabbages, which provided much needed vitamins and a welcome change in their diet.

Despite their adaptation, the threat of outside discovery always loomed. They were acutely aware that their enemies, those who had sought to destroy the Order, might follow them across the ocean. The knowledge that they held precious relics entrusted to their care fuelled their determination to remain undetected. They spent many hours refining their defensive strategies; booby traps were laid around their settlement, and a network of hidden trails and lookouts was established. The brothers, seasoned warriors, were always on high alert. Every rustle in the undergrowth, every unfamiliar shadow, sent a ripple of fear and vigilance through the community.

The brothers' resilience was tested not only by the harsh environment and the ever-present danger of discovery, but also by the psychological toll of exile. The loss of their brothers and the destruction of their order in Europe weighed heavily on their hearts. The solace they found in their shared faith, in their brotherhood, was a lifeline, keeping them anchored in their identity and preventing them from succumbing to despair. They held regular services, their voices rising in hymns of hope and resilience, their prayers echoing through the forest. These weren't merely religious observances; they were acts of communal healing,

reaffirmations of their unity, and expressions of their

enduring spirit. The community, forged in the fires of

adversity, became a sanctuary, a refuge where they could find strength in each other's company.

Building a new community demanded innovation and

creativity. The brothers, accustomed to the structured life of the Templar Order, had to reinvent themselves. They learned new skills, adapting their existing knowledge to the demands of their new environment. Their military training proved surprisingly useful in hunting and defense, while their organizational skills facilitated the management of their resources. The brothers who had excelled in accounting and logistics now managed the community's stores, ensuring the equitable distribution of food and supplies. The former scribes meticulously documented their experiences, recording their struggles and triumphs in painstaking detail, creating a testament to their resilience and ingenuity. Each brother, regardless of their past rank, contributed to the collective effort, their skills and experience woven together to create a functional and self-sufficient society.

Their relationship with the Mi'kmaq, the indigenous people of Nova Scotia, was initially cautious. The Templars, experienced in dealing with diverse cultures in the Holy Land, approached the interaction with respect and diplomacy. They sought to avoid conflict and instead to build relationships based on mutual understanding. This wasn't easy. Language barriers proved challenging, and cultural differences often led to misunderstandings. But the brothers patiently learned from the Mi'kmaq, observing their hunting techniques, their methods of food preservation, and their deep knowledge of the land. They were not just seeking to survive; they were also seeking to learn and adapt, demonstrating their open-mindedness and their respect for a culture vastly different from their own.

The nights were long and often filled with the haunting calls of owls and the rustling of unknown creatures. Fear, a constant companion, was tempered by the warmth of shared companionship. They gathered around crackling fires, sharing stories and memories from their past lives. The weight of their losses was a heavy burden, but the brothers supported each other, providing comfort and solace. They talked of Jerusalem, of their comrades lost, of the injustices they had faced. But as the nights grew longer, their conversation slowly shifted towards the future, towards the hope of establishing a lasting sanctuary in this unforgiving yet beautiful land. The fires, casting their warm glow on their faces, symbolized not just their physical warmth but also the unwavering flame of hope that burned within them. The harsh conditions of their exile gradually molded them into a stronger, more resilient community, more united in faith and purpose, more resolute in their mission to protect their sacred heritage. The wilderness, once a symbol of their isolation and hardship, was slowly becoming a testament to their indomitable spirit, and their unwavering capacity to forge a new life from the ruins of their old. Their journey was far from over; the seeds of their new community had been sown, but the harvest remained to be seen.

Conflict and Resolution

The second winter proved even more challenging than the first. The initial euphoria of building their longhouses and establishing a semblance of order had faded, replaced by a gnawing weariness and a creeping sense of isolation. The endless grey skies, the biting winds, and the relentless snow seemed to mirror the turmoil brewing within their ranks.

Brother Jean-Luc, a veteran of countless battles, found himself increasingly irritable, his usually jovial nature replaced by a brooding silence. The endless toil, the constant struggle for survival, had eroded his patience, and he often clashed with Brother Thomas over logistical matters, his criticisms laced with a bitterness that stung. Thomas, ever the pragmatist, bore his rebukes with quiet dignity, but the friction between them was palpable, casting a shadow over the fragile brotherhood.

The disagreements weren't confined to Jean-Luc and Thomas. The constant pressure of their situation, the knowledge that they were fugitives, hunted by the might of the French crown and the papal inquisition, gnawed at the men. Old rivalries, long dormant, resurfaced, fueled by exhaustion and the gnawing fear of discovery. Brother Guillaume, usually a pillar of calm and reason, found himself consumed by anxieties, his faith shaken by the seemingly endless hardships. He questioned the wisdom of their flight, wondering if they should have surrendered, accepted their fate, rather than enduring this grueling exile. His doubts, though unspoken, hung heavy in the air, a poison slowly infecting the community's morale.

One particularly harsh evening, as a blizzard raged outside, the tension finally erupted. During their evening meal of meager broth and dried beans, a heated argument broke out between Jean-Luc and Brother Etienne, a young Templar who had shown remarkable courage and resilience throughout their ordeal. Etienne, exhausted from a day of hunting, had made a careless remark about Jean-Luc's leadership, accusing him of being overly cautious and indecisive. Jean-Luc, already simmering with frustration, exploded, his voice booming across the longhouse. Words were exchanged, harsh and unforgiving, revealing long-held resentments and simmering frustrations. The other brothers watched, their faces etched with apprehension, as the two men traded insults, their voices escalating into a furious clash.

The argument threatened to escalate into a physical

confrontation, a prospect that horrified the others. Brother Anselm, a gentle soul with a calming presence, intervened, his voice clear and steady amidst the storm of accusations.

He reminded them of their shared faith, of their vows, of their commitment to protecting the sacred relics entrusted to their care. He spoke of the sacrifices they had already made, of the common goal that bound them together. His words, simple yet powerful, pierced through the animosity, gradually calming the heated exchange.

The intervention, however, was only a temporary reprieve. The underlying tensions remained, a constant threat to their fragile unity. Grand Master Geoffroi, a man of quiet strength and unwavering faith, recognized the danger. He called a meeting, urging the brothers to confront their issues openly and honestly. He reminded them that their survival depended on their unity, that internal strife would prove as deadly as any external enemy.

The meeting was fraught with emotion. Each brother, in turn, confessed their fears, anxieties, and frustrations. Jean-Luc admitted his impatience and his struggle to adapt to the harsh realities of their new life. Guillaume confessed his doubts, his wavering faith, expressing the weight of their seemingly unending ordeal. Etienne apologized for his disrespectful outburst, acknowledging his own exhaustion and the strain it had placed on his temper. The open confession, the act of vulnerability, proved cathartic. The brothers listened, offering support and understanding, a testament to the enduring bond forged in the crucible of their shared

adversity.

Following the heart-to-heart, a plan was formulated to

address their issues collectively. Tasks were reassigned to better utilize each brother's skills and temperaments, easing the burden on those who were struggling. A new system of communal responsibility was introduced, ensuring that everyone contributed to the daily necessities, fostering a greater sense of shared purpose. Regular prayer services and reflective discussions were implemented to reinforce their faith and their common bond. Brother Anselm, with his soothing presence and wisdom, became a vital mediator, helping to resolve conflicts and mediate disagreements before they escalated.

The shift was gradual but noticeable. The atmosphere within the longhouse became less tense, more harmonious. The brothers, having faced their internal demons, found a renewed sense of camaraderie. They found comfort in the simple acts of shared labor, in the quiet moments of prayer, in the stories they exchanged around the fire. The wilderness, once a symbol of their isolation and hardship, now became a crucible where their faith, their perseverance, and their brotherhood were tested and ultimately strengthened.

The challenge of their exile, however, wasn't limited to internal conflict. External threats also loomed. The

Mi'kmaq, initially wary of the newcomers, remained a

source of both potential conflict and assistance. The brothers carefully navigated the delicate balance, offering gifts and showing respect, gradually fostering a level of trust. There were instances of misunderstanding, of cultural clashes, but through patience and diplomacy, they managed to avoid open hostility. They learned to rely on the Mi'kmaq's knowledge of the land, their expertise in hunting and trapping, their understanding of the harsh environment. The indigenous people, in turn, were gradually won over by the Templars' discipline, their unwavering faith, and their willingness to work alongside them. The exchange was not always easy, but it proved mutually beneficial. The Templars learned to survive in this new environment, while the Mi'kmaq found a reliable trading partner, and a group of unexpected allies.

Their greatest fear, however, remained the possibility of discovery. Rumors of their presence, whispers carried on the wind, reached their ears. They knew that their sanctuary was not truly secure, that their secret couldn't remain hidden forever. The weight of their past, the ever-present threat of discovery, spurred them to work tirelessly to secure their hiding place, reinforcing their defenses, ensuring that their sacred treasure remained hidden from any prying eyes. They worked with renewed vigor, their shared purpose uniting them in the face of their common danger. Each brother played his part, from the meticulous booby-traps set by Brother Thomas, to the intricate camouflage developed by Brother Etienne, who had an innate understanding of blending into the natural environment.

Their exile, though arduous, was slowly shaping them into something new. The wilderness, once a symbol of their despair and isolation, was forging them into a resilient and cohesive brotherhood, a community bound by faith,

adversity, and a shared mission. The conflicts they had

overcome, the challenges they had faced, had strengthened their bonds, revealing the true depth of their commitment to each other and to their sacred trust. The seeds of their new community, sown in hardship and nurtured by adversity, were finally taking root, promising a future that, while uncertain, held the possibility of enduring strength and spiritual resilience. Their journey was far from over, but they had weathered the storms, both internal and external,

emerging stronger and more united than ever before. The future remained uncertain, but their hope, their faith, and their brotherhood burned bright, casting a warm glow in the heart of the unforgiving wilderness.

Spiritual Strength

The biting wind howled a mournful dirge through the skeletal branches of the pines, a constant reminder of their isolation. Yet, within the rough-hewn walls of their longhouses, a different kind of strength was taking hold. It wasn't the brute force of arms, honed on the battlefields of the Holy Land, but a quieter, deeper strength, born of faith and unwavering perseverance. Brother Thomas, his face etched with the lines of hardship, led the evening prayers.

His voice, though weary, held a resolute strength that resonated through the small community. The flickering candlelight danced across the faces of his brothers,

illuminating their weathered features, their eyes reflecting both the harsh realities of their exile and the unwavering light of their faith.

Their daily rituals, once performed with the practiced ease of men accustomed to the grandeur of Templar life, were now imbued with a raw, primal significance. The simple act of saying Mass, once a formal ceremony conducted in magnificent cathedrals, now took on a profound sacredness within the cramped confines of their longhouse. Every word, every gesture, every intonation was laden with the weight of their survival, their hope, and their desperate clinging to the tenets of their faith. It was a faith that had been tested,

stretched to its limits, but never broken.

Brother Etienne, a scholar by nature, had meticulously

preserved the few remaining texts salvaged from their flight.

His hands, roughened by the relentless toil, moved with reverence as he carefully turned the fragile pages, his voice a low murmur as he read passages from the scriptures. His words, filled with comfort and solace, served as a balm to their weary souls. He wasn't merely reciting words; he was reminding them of the promises made, of the strength found in the divine grace, of the unwavering belief that their suffering was not without purpose.

Their spiritual resilience wasn't simply a matter of individual piety; it was woven into the very fabric of their community.

They shared their meager rations, their burdens, and their hopes, forging a bond that was as strong as any fortress. Brother Jean-Luc, whose initial bitterness had threatened to shatter their fragile unity, slowly began to find solace in their shared devotion. He participated in the prayers with a newfound fervor, his gruff voice joining the chorus of hymns that echoed through the longhouse, a testament to the transformative power of shared faith.

The wilderness, initially a symbol of their despair, gradually became a source of spiritual reflection. They found themselves drawn to the natural world, finding parallels in the resilience of the towering pines and the tenacity of the tenacious wildflowers pushing through the snow. The vastness of the landscape mirrored the immensity of their faith, reminding them that even in the face of overwhelming odds, there was still hope. They learned to find God in the quiet majesty of the forest, in the crashing waves of the Atlantic, and in the unwavering strength of their shared fellowship.

The long, dark nights were filled with whispered prayers, with stories from their past, and with discussions of theology that helped them navigate the complexities of their situation. They debated the meaning of their exile, the reasons for their suffering, and the possible paths that lay ahead. These discussions were not merely intellectual exercises; they were crucial to their spiritual survival. They were a testament to the enduring strength of their faith and their commitment to the Templar ideals.

The annual observance of Easter took on a particularly profound significance that year. The celebration wasn't marked by grand processions or elaborate rituals, but by a simple act of communion, shared in quiet solemnity within their makeshift chapel. Brother Geoffroy, usually the most jovial of their number, recounted the story of Christ's resurrection with a deep emotion that moved all those present to tears. He spoke of the triumph over adversity, of the power of faith and hope, even in the darkest of times, drawing parallels to their own journey. The humble

celebration was a potent symbol of their resilience, their faith, and their enduring belief in a better future.

Their shared faith helped them overcome numerous

challenges. The constant threat of starvation, the harsh weather conditions, and the lurking fear of discovery all loomed large, but their spiritual resilience stood as an

impenetrable shield. They supported each other, prayed for strength and guidance, and found renewed purpose in their mission to safeguard their sacred trust. Their prayers weren't just pleas for divine intervention; they were affirmations of their commitment, their unwavering resolve, and their unyielding hope.

One evening, while Brother Etienne recounted the life of Saint Bernard of Clairvaux, Brother Jean-Luc posed a

question that reflected the turmoil within many hearts:

"Brother Etienne, if God is all-powerful, why does He allow us to suffer so?" His question hung heavy in the air, a testament to the growing doubt that occasionally gnawed at their faith. Etienne, after a moment of quiet contemplation, responded with a profound wisdom that transcended the simple answer. He spoke of the refining power of suffering, of the way trials could strengthen and purify the spirit, and of the importance of accepting God's will, even when it was difficult to comprehend. He reminded them that even Christ himself had endured unimaginable suffering, and yet through his sacrifice, he brought forth the greatest of triumphs. His words brought a sense of peace, reaffirming their shared belief that even in their suffering, there was a divine purpose.

Their faith wasn't simply a passive acceptance of their fate; it was an active force that fueled their determination and inspired their actions. They worked tirelessly, not only to ensure their survival but also to build a life that reflected their values. They established a small garden, cultivating herbs and vegetables to supplement their meager diet, finding in this simple act of creation a deeper connection to the earth and to their faith. They crafted tools and built structures, transforming the raw materials of the forest into functional and beautiful objects, a testament to their resilience and ingenuity.

As time passed, the wilderness, initially a daunting challenge, became a sanctuary. It wasn't just a place of refuge, but a place where their faith flourished, a place where they found a deeper understanding of themselves, of each other, and of their relationship with God. The vastness of the landscape, once a symbol of their isolation, became a reminder of the boundless nature of divine love. The solitude of the forest became a space for quiet contemplation and spiritual reflection. Their spiritual strength, nourished by adversity and tempered by faith, became their most powerful weapon. It enabled them to face any challenge, internal or external, that lay ahead on their arduous journey. The wilderness, initially a desolate prison, had inadvertently become a crucible, forging them into a brotherhood whose bonds were stronger than steel, their faith brighter than any earthly treasure. Their journey of survival was far from over, but in the heart of the unforgiving wilderness, they had found a strength that would sustain them through all their trials, a spiritual resilience that was as enduring as the land itself.

Relations with Natives

The first encounter had been tentative, a silent observation from behind thickets of pine and birch. They, the remnants of the once-mighty Templar Order, had watched from afar as a small band of Mi'kmaq emerged from the depths of the forest, their movements fluid and graceful, a stark contrast to their own stiff, battle-worn postures. Fear, a familiar companion, had initially held sway, but curiosity, a potent emotion even amidst despair, had ultimately won. The Mi'kmaq, clad in furs and adorned with intricate beadwork, seemed as wary of them as they were of the newcomers. Days turned into weeks, punctuated by cautious approaches and hesitant gestures. Brother Etienne, always the most observant, noted the Mi'kmaq's reliance on the land, their intricate understanding of its rhythms and secrets. Their hunting prowess was legendary, their knowledge of

medicinal herbs astonishing.

One day, a young Mi'kmaq boy, no older than ten, ventured close to their makeshift camp. He was drawn by the aroma of roasting venison, a familiar scent but prepared in a manner unfamiliar to him. He approached cautiously, eyes wide with a mixture of fear and fascination. Brother Giles, whose patience had been tested many times during their arduous flight, offered the boy a piece of roasted meat. The boy hesitated, then, with a surprising gesture of trust, took the offering and ate it slowly. This single act, seemingly insignificant, became the first bridge between two worlds.

Slowly, cautiously, communication began. It wasn't a smooth process. Gestures, rudimentary drawings in the sand, and the universal language of shared meals helped break down the barriers of language and mistrust. They learned that the

Mi'kmaq, or "Míkmaq" as they pronounced it themselves, were not the savage hordes depicted in the tales of European explorers. They were a people deeply connected to their land, their spirituality intertwined with the natural world.

They revered the animals they hunted, offering prayers of gratitude before consuming their bounty. They possessed a profound understanding of herbal remedies, their knowledge surpassing anything the Templars had encountered in Europe.

The Mi'kmaq, in turn, learned about the Templars, not as bloodthirsty crusaders, but as men fleeing persecution,

seeking sanctuary in a foreign land. They learned of the Templars' unwavering faith, their loyalty to one another, and the sacred burden they carried – a burden they guarded with fierce determination. The Mi'kmaq were a people of strong spiritual beliefs, respecting the strength of their faith, though it was different from their own. Their shared spirituality, though expressed differently, formed a common ground that helped foster mutual understanding. The Templars learned the Mi'kmaq language slowly but surely, using simple phrases and drawings. Their progress was surprisingly rapid, fueled by their mutual desire for communication and

survival.

The sharing of knowledge and resources became a crucial aspect of their co-existence. The Templars, skilled in

metalworking and construction, taught the Mi'kmaq new techniques, improving their tools and building materials. In return, the Mi'kmaq shared their knowledge of the land, teaching the Templars how to hunt, fish, and identify edible plants. They showed them the best trapping locations, the most fruitful fishing grounds, and the safest places to shelter during harsh weather conditions. Brother Thomas, known for his calm demeanor and keen intellect, quickly adapted to this new life. He proved a capable hunter, becoming adept at using the Mi'kmaq's techniques, while his knowledge of herbal remedies proved invaluable in treating ailments. His prayers were no longer merely whispered within the walls of their longhouses, but occasionally offered out under the expansive canopy of the forest, a blend of Christian and indigenous spirituality rising together on the evening breeze.

The exchange wasn't merely practical; it fostered a growing sense of mutual respect and even friendship. The Templars, initially haunted by the ghosts of their past, began to find solace in the Mi'kmaq's peaceful existence, their reverence for the land, and their strong community bonds. They witnessed the Mi'kmaq's deep respect for elders and their meticulous care for the young. They observed their intricate storytelling traditions, each tale a lesson in history, survival, and the importance of community. The stories filled the long winter nights, bridging cultural differences and weaving a tapestry of shared experience.

One notable aspect of their collaboration was the Mi'kmaq's uncanny ability to navigate the wilderness. Their understanding of the terrain and its hidden trails was extraordinary, surpassing the Templars' knowledge of European landscapes. This proved invaluable as they moved their hidden treasure, carefully selecting the site to build their subterranean vault for their precious relics. The Mi'kmaq's assistance was vital in transporting the materials they needed for the construction and ensuring the secrecy of their location. Trust became crucial in this collaboration, and both sides found a shared strength in their commitment.

The mutual assistance extended beyond practical matters.

The Mi'kmaq's understanding of the wilderness, coupled with their medical knowledge, proved incredibly beneficial in treating injuries and illnesses. Their herbal remedies, often based on centuries of traditional practices, complemented the

Templars' limited medical knowledge, ensuring the survival and wellbeing of the community.

However, the relationship was not without its challenges. Cultural differences sometimes led to misunderstandings and conflicts. The Templars' rigid hierarchical structure clashed, at times, with the Mi'kmaq's more egalitarian society.

Differences in religious beliefs presented occasional friction, but their shared commitment to community and mutual respect prevailed over their disagreements. Their differing perceptions of land ownership, a concept almost alien to the Mi'kmaq worldview, required delicate navigation. Yet, through patience, mutual respect, and a willingness to compromise, these differences were often addressed before they escalated into significant conflicts.

The relationship between the Templars and the Mi'kmaq evolved from a tentative alliance to a genuine partnership. The harsh realities of their shared existence in the wilderness forged a bond stronger than any treaty or agreement. The Mi'kmaq's deep connection to the land, their resilience, and their unwavering spiritual faith enriched the Templars' lives in unexpected ways. They discovered that survival was not merely a matter of physical strength, but of mutual support, understanding, and respect for the diverse tapestry of humanity. The wilderness, once a symbol of exile and isolation, had become a crucible of inter-cultural understanding and cooperation, transforming two seemingly disparate cultures into a vibrant and resilient community. The survival of the last Templars in the new world depended not only on their faith and military skills but on the

unexpected alliances and shared destinies forged in the

unforgiving landscape of Nova Scotia. The wilderness, initially a barrier, was becoming an unexpected bridge to a new life and a different future. The journey into the heart of the wilderness became a journey into the heart of humanity.

Rumors and Spies

The biting Nova Scotian wind whipped through the sparse trees, carrying with it not only the chill of the late autumn air but also whispers, insidious and unsettling. Weeks had passed since the Templars had landed on these shores, weeks spent carving a sanctuary from the unforgiving wilderness.

The initial relief of escape from the relentless pursuit in Europe had begun to fade, replaced by a gnawing unease. Their precarious existence, built on secrecy and the hope of oblivion, felt increasingly fragile.

The first whispers arrived not through any direct threat, but via the wind itself, borne on the ragged edges of rumors that drifted across the vast expanse of the Atlantic. Fishermen, their faces weathered by sun and salt, would occasionally venture close to their hidden encampment, their words laced with caution and hushed tones. They spoke of the Pope's decree, of the relentless hunt for the Order, a hunt that had spread like wildfire across Europe. The stories were fragmented, often contradictory, fueled by fear and speculation, yet they carried an undercurrent of chilling truth. The world still sought the Templars, and the whispers suggested their survival was not as secret as they had hoped.

Brother Thomas, a seasoned Templar with a keen eye for detail and an even keener ear, had taken it upon himself to monitor these whispers. He possessed a natural talent for gathering intelligence, a skill honed over years of navigating the treacherous political landscape of the Crusades. He spent hours listening to the fishermen, subtly guiding their conversations, extracting fragments of information, piecing together the puzzle of their pursuers. He learned that the Inquisition, far from being content with the initial purge in

Europe, was extending its reach, its long tendrils snaking across the ocean, searching for any trace of the surviving Templars.

The stories also spoke of bounty hunters, mercenaries hired by wealthy nobles eager to claim the rumored Templar treasures, attracted by the legend of their immense wealth. These men were not bound by any religious zeal; they were driven by avarice, their loyalty bought and sold with gold. The very thought of these ruthless mercenaries hunting them like animals sent shivers down the spines of even the most seasoned knights.

Adding to the unease were the rumors of spies, shadowy figures operating in the fringes of society. Brother Thomas suspected that the Inquisition had already planted its agents in Nova Scotia, individuals posing as traders, settlers, or even missionaries, their true purpose masked by a veneer of normalcy. Their presence was a constant threat, a cold dread hanging in the air, making the silence of the forest seem to crackle with unseen eyes and listening ears.

The Templars, ever mindful of their vulnerability,

established a rudimentary system of surveillance. Sentinels were posted at strategic locations around their hidden sanctuary, their eyes constantly scanning the horizon, their ears attuned to any unusual sound. Brother Jean-Luc, a younger knight renowned for his agility and stealth, was tasked with scouting the surrounding area, his movements as silent as the fall of autumn leaves. He would venture out under the cover of darkness, venturing far into the wilderness, his only company the whispering wind and the watchful eyes of the moon. He returned with reports of unusual activity: unfamiliar tracks in the snow, the glint of distant campfires, whispered conversations carried on the night breeze, all hinting at unseen eyes and potential threats.

Their initial encounters with the Mi'kmaq, the indigenous people of the land, had been cautious, marked by a mutual suspicion. However, as time passed, a tentative

understanding had begun to emerge. The Templars, with their skills in craftsmanship and medicine, had proven

themselves to be valuable allies. They shared knowledge, exchanging goods and services – the Templars providing tools and medicines, the Mi'kmaq offering knowledge of the land, its hidden paths and its resources. This developing trust, though fragile, was a vital asset. It offered the Templars a lifeline to intelligence, an insight into the movements of outsiders, and perhaps, crucially, a chance to forge alliances against a common enemy.

One particularly frigid evening, a Mi'kmaq elder, known for his wisdom and connection to the spirits, approached Brother Thomas. His eyes, deep and knowing, held a certain weight, a gravity that spoke of secrets carried through generations. He spoke of whispers, rumors reaching even into the heart of their isolated villages, whispers of men searching for the "lost sons of God," – the Templars. The elder spoke of sightings, of unfamiliar ships anchored in distant bays, and of heavily armed men traveling through the forests, their faces hidden beneath hooded cloaks.

This information was crucial, confirming Brother Thomas's worst fears. The Inquisition, or at least its agents, were closing in. The bounty hunters were already here, operating in secrecy, their presence an ominous shadow hanging over the fragile peace the Templars had established.

The news stirred a wave of anxiety within the Templar

community. The initial euphoria of escape had been replaced by a desperate awareness of their vulnerability. Their sanctuary, once a haven of peace, now felt like a cage, surrounded by the ever-tightening coils of pursuit. The brothers began to strengthen their defenses, enhancing their existing booby traps and constructing more robust barriers around their encampment. They sharpened their weapons, their training sessions growing more intense, the air thick with a sense of foreboding.

The quiet, contemplative prayers that had once characterized their lives were now punctuated by hushed discussions of strategy, the solemn murmur of plans laid against an uncertain future. The very air itself seemed charged with anticipation, the weight of impending danger pressing down on them, a palpable sense of unease that mirrored the anxieties churning within their hearts. The whispers had become shouts, the rumors a cacophony, and the shadows of their pursuers loomed larger with each passing day, transforming their secluded haven into a precarious battleground for survival. Their faith, their brotherhood, and their resourcefulness would be tested to their very limits.

The whispers of pursuit had become a roar, and the chase was on. The tranquility of their sanctuary was about to be shattered, and the fight for their lives, and for the sacred relics entrusted to their care, was about to begin.

Gathering Intelligence

The crackling fire cast long, dancing shadows across the faces of the assembled Knights. Brother Thomas, his

normally jovial face etched with grim determination,

addressed them. "Our sanctuary, brothers, while seemingly isolated, is not impervious. The whispers of our arrival, though faint, have undoubtedly reached ears beyond these shores. We must know who watches us, and what they seek."

A murmur rippled through the group. Brother Geoffrey, a veteran of countless battles, spoke, his voice low and gravelly. "We cannot afford to be complacent. The King of France, Philip, spared no expense in hunting us down in Europe. He will not rest until he reclaims the relics."

Brother Etienne, a younger knight, but sharp of mind,

offered a counterpoint. "But if he knows where we are, why hasn't he struck already? Perhaps this silence is a calculated move, designed to lull us into a false sense of security."

Brother Thomas nodded, his gaze sweeping over the faces of his brethren. "Etienne is right. Silence can be as deadly as an open assault. We need to ascertain their plans before they act. We need intelligence." He paused, considering. "We need eyes and ears beyond our immediate circle."

Their previous methods of survival – hunting, foraging, and constructing their rudimentary defenses – would not suffice.

This was a new kind of struggle, a war of shadows and whispers, demanding a new approach. They needed a system, a network of informants, however tenuous.

Their first step was to recruit. Their isolated existence, while initially a blessing, now posed a challenge. They were reliant on their own resources and skills, with no network of local contacts to tap into. This meant approaching their survival differently. They needed individuals who could blend into the wilderness, gathering information without arousing

suspicion. Their first option was engaging with the

indigenous Mi'kmaq people.

Approaching the Mi'kmaq required tact and respect. The Templars understood the importance of diplomacy,

particularly considering their precarious position. Brother Alain, known for his gentle spirit and ability to learn languages, was entrusted with this delicate task. He spent days observing the Mi'kmaq villages from a distance, studying their customs and their patterns of movement. He then chose to offer gifts, not as a form of bribery, but as a gesture of peaceful intentions. He brought carefully crafted tools, not weapons, showing his respect for their way of life and creating opportunities for interaction and exchange.

Over several weeks, Alain patiently built trust, exchanging simple pleasantries and demonstrating the Templars' goodwill through acts of kindness and generosity. He discovered that the Mi'kmaq, while aware of the strange newcomers in their lands, held no hostility toward them. They were primarily concerned with their own survival and the preservation of their ancestral lands. The news of the Templars' arrival had reached them through passing traders. The vague whispers spoke of a group of devout men who lived in the woods, seeking peace and quiet. Nothing more.

Alain's success provided a vital first step. Through his interactions, he uncovered a loose network of communication that stretched across various Mi'kmaq villages. The whispers about the Templars, initially scattered and indistinct, now became more focused. They learned of occasional sightings of unfamiliar ships along the coast, ships that lingered suspiciously close to the shore before sailing away. Alain also discovered a pattern: the ships consistently appeared around the full moon, suggesting a planned and deliberate approach.

The next phase of their intelligence gathering required a different approach. The Templars knew they needed

someone who could venture beyond the immediate area, someone who could navigate the treacherous coastal waters and blend in with the sparse maritime communities along the Nova Scotia coastline. Brother Jean, a skilled navigator and a man of quiet resolve, was tasked with this perilous

mission.

Jean, equipped with a small, sturdy fishing vessel disguised to appear inconspicuous, ventured out onto the unforgiving Atlantic. He targeted small fishing villages, posing as a lone fisherman seeking trade and supplies. His weathered appearance and mastery of seafaring skills helped him to blend in seamlessly. He spent weeks navigating the treacherous currents and navigating the wary eyes of the villagers, establishing connections and gathering information in exchange for some of his carefully saved provisions.

Jean's clandestine journeys revealed a more troubling

picture. He learned of sightings of foreign ships, descriptions that matched the ones Alain had already gathered. He learned of hushed conversations in taverns, rumors that spoke of a "powerful lord" seeking some kind of "ancient treasure" hidden in the wilderness. Jean's insights confirmed the Templars' worst fears: their sanctuary was not as isolated as they had initially believed. The whispers of their pursuit were rapidly transforming into concrete threats. A systematic search was underway.

The information gathered by Alain and Jean was invaluable.

It painted a disturbing picture, hinting at a well-organized and relentless pursuit. They now possessed clues to the identity of their pursuers, their methods, and their likely objectives. This knowledge, hard-won through painstaking efforts, allowed the Templars to prepare their defenses, strengthening their fortifications, and devising new strategies to safeguard their secrets and their lives. The whispers had been answered, and the game of survival had entered a new, more dangerous phase. The silence, once a comfort, now echoed with the chilling knowledge of approaching danger, a reminder of the relentless pursuit that still awaited them.

Their fight for survival had just begun, and the shadows of the relentless pursuit stretched long before them. The

relentless pursuit was not a whisper anymore; it was a roar echoing in the depths of the wilderness, threatening to engulf them. The race for their survival had reached a critical juncture. Their faith, their brotherhood, and their resolve would be tested like never before. The fate of the holy relics and their own lives hung precariously in the balance. The struggle had become a desperate dance between survival and destruction, a relentless chase across the untamed wilderness, a fight for survival against the looming shadow of an inescapable destiny.

Unexpected Allies

The biting Nova Scotian wind whipped around Brother Alain as he surveyed the desolate landscape. The recent snowfall had blanketed the forest in a pristine white, but the beauty was deceptive. Beneath the serene surface, the threat of pursuit gnawed at their peace. Jean, his ever-vigilant companion, stood beside him, his gaze scanning the horizon.

The whispers of their presence, once a faint murmur, had escalated into a persistent hum, a growing unease that chilled them to the bone.

Their immediate concern wasn't just the organized force hunting them; it was the unknown. The vast, unforgiving wilderness offered both sanctuary and peril. The local

Mi'kmaq people, with their intimate knowledge of the land, held the key to survival—or to their undoing. Alain and Jean had encountered scattered Mi'kmaq settlements during their travels, observing their cautious interactions with the outside world. The Templars were wary, understanding that revealing their true identity could bring both aid and destruction.

One evening, while foraging for supplies near a small river, they stumbled upon a group of Mi'kmaq women gathering herbs. Fear, initially, was palpable. The Templars, clad in their worn, adapted clothing, were a stark contrast to the indigenous people's simple attire. But instead of hostile action, a cautious curiosity settled over the women. Alain, remembering the few words of Mi'kmaq he had painstakingly learned from a tattered book found amongst the Templar archives, attempted a greeting. His pronunciation was clumsy, his grammar atrocious, yet the intent was clear.

To their astonishment, one of the women responded in

broken French. A hesitant conversation began, punctuated by gestures and shared smiles. The women, it transpired, were aware of the strangers' presence. Their knowledge wasn't gleaned from simple observation, however. Rumors, whispered through the interconnected network of their communities, spoke of "men of God," seeking refuge, hunted by unseen enemies. The implication was not lost on Alain and Jean; their secret was, in part, already known.

The women, whose names were revealed to be Anya, Tala, and Keisha, expressed a deep-seated mistrust of the outside world—a world that had repeatedly broken promises and encroached on their land. However, they were far from indifferent to the suffering of others. Their empathy, born from years of hardship and struggle, resonated with the Templars' plight. They understood the concept of being hunted, of being forced to flee for survival. A shared bond of resilience began to form, a bridge built across cultural

divides.

Over the following weeks, the trust deepened. The Mi'kmaq women provided invaluable assistance, not only with food and shelter but also with crucial information. They shared their knowledge of the terrain, revealing hidden trails and safe havens that were invisible to outsiders. They warned of the scouts, the men who were systematically searching the region; men whose faces were shrouded in mystery but whose ruthlessness was evident.

Anya, the eldest of the three, proved to be exceptionally insightful. She possessed a keen understanding of human nature and an uncanny ability to read the subtle signs that revealed the truth. Her understanding of the forest's secrets was matched only by her intuitive grasp of unspoken language. She revealed that the pursuit wasn't solely focused on the Templars; it was intertwined with a complex web of political intrigue, involving powerful figures who sought to exploit the situation for their personal gain. This knowledge gave the Templars a new perspective. Their fight for survival was not an isolated incident, but a pawn in a larger, far more dangerous game.

Tala, a skilled hunter, kept vigil, tracking the movement of the pursuers, relaying their findings to the Templars through a series of carefully placed signals. Her knowledge of the forest's rhythms and the subtle tracks left by the intruders enabled her to anticipate their movements, helping the Templars to avoid direct confrontation. Her agility and knowledge allowed for better planning and strategies for the survival of the Knights. She was the eyes and ears of the small group, allowing for timely responses to emerging threats and maintaining a level of awareness that was

otherwise unimaginable.

Keisha, the youngest of the three, possessed an extraordinary talent for communication. She spoke to other members of her tribe, spreading a carefully constructed narrative that deflected attention from the Templars' actual location. Her words weaved a tapestry of misdirection and rumor, creating a smokescreen to conceal their true whereabouts. She carefully used the already existing rumors of men of god seeking refuge, carefully adding detail to make them less conspicuous.

This unlikely alliance became the foundation of the

Templars' survival. The Knights, masters of strategy and combat, complemented the Mi'kmaq women's intimate knowledge of the land and their intuitive grasp of the local politics. Their collaboration was not just a matter of practicality; it was a testament to the unexpected bonds that could be forged in times of adversity. The seemingly insurmountable odds seemed a bit less daunting with the help of their newfound allies.

One day, a group of heavily armed men, clearly European soldiers, appeared near the Templars' hidden camp. The situation was precarious. The numbers were heavily stacked against the Templars. But Tala, having anticipated their arrival through her vigilant tracking, had prepared an ambush. The Mi'kmaq women, utilizing their knowledge of the terrain, directed the Templars into a strategic position, launching a surprise attack that drove the soldiers back. The soldiers, unprepared for the fierce resistance, were forced to retreat, leaving behind several fallen comrades. The victory, though small, was a testament to the effectiveness of their newfound partnership.

The unexpected alliance with the Mi'kmaq women

transformed the Templars' struggle. It wasn't just about survival anymore; it was about forging a new path, a new understanding of community and resilience. The shared struggles forged an unlikely bond of trust and respect,

blurring the lines of culture and faith. It was a silent

testament to the shared human spirit that transcended

boundaries. The whispers of pursuit continued, but the

Templars were no longer isolated. They had found allies, and with their help, they possessed a newfound hope in their desperate fight for survival. The landscape, once a symbol of isolation, now represented the potential for unexpected strength and survival, a testament to the power of shared adversity. The harsh reality of their situation did not diminish, but the shared knowledge and resources provided a measure of confidence that was crucial for their survival.

The unexpected allies offered more than just intelligence; they offered hope – a beacon in the dark, uncertain future.

The First Attack

The first sign was the snapping of a twig, far too crisp for the gentle snowfall. Jean, ever alert, nudged Alain. His hand, calloused and weathered from years of swordplay and toil, rested lightly on the hilt of his worn sword. The silence that followed was thick with tension, a palpable weight pressing down on the small Templar encampment nestled within the protective embrace of the ancient pines. The Mi'kmaq women, their faces etched with concern, moved closer to their makeshift shelters, their eyes mirroring the apprehension that gripped the Templars.

The second sign came swiftly, a flurry of movement at the edge of the treeline, the glint of steel catching the fading light. A volley of arrows whistled through the air, the sharp thwack of wood against flesh echoing through the clearing.

One of the Mi'kmaq women cried out, clutching at her shoulder as a shaft protruded from her arm. The unexpected attack was swift and brutal, a calculated ambush executed with precision and deadly efficiency.

Alain roared a command, his voice cutting through the

chaos. The Templars, though outnumbered, reacted with practiced efficiency. Their years of training kicked in,

transforming the small encampment into a whirlwind of steel and determination. Swords clashed against crude axes and spears, the air filled with the grunts of exertion and the agonized cries of the wounded. Jean, a whirlwind of motion, deflected an axe blow aimed at one of the Mi'kmaq women, his sword a blur of silver. Alain, his movements more measured but no less deadly, dispatched his attackers with swift, precise strikes, his eyes constantly scanning for new threats.

The attackers were not professional soldiers, but their

ferocity and knowledge of the terrain were undeniable. They fought with the desperate desperation of men pushed to the brink, their movements fueled by a hatred that bordered on religious fanaticism. Were these mere bandits, or something more sinister? The question gnawed at Alain, even amidst the chaos of the battle. He recognized in their ferocity a disturbing echo of the religious zeal that had driven the Crusades, a blind faith twisted into a weapon of violence.

The fight raged for what felt like an eternity. The snow, once pristine, was now stained crimson, the air thick with the coppery tang of blood. Despite their initial surprise, the Templars and their Mi'kmaq allies fought back with courage and skill, their combined strength exceeding the sum of their individual parts. The bond forged through shared hardship proved its worth, a testament to their burgeoning alliance. The women fought with a ferocity that belied their apparent fragility, their screams of battle echoing the cries of their ancestors. They were warriors, defending their home, their way of life, and their newfound allies.

As the sun dipped below the horizon, casting long shadows across the battlefield, the tide began to turn. The attackers, exhausted and demoralized by the Templars' unwavering resistance, began to falter. One by one, they fell, their bodies adding to the grim tableau of the conflict. The final attacker, a burly man with eyes filled with a burning hatred, lunged at Alain with a desperate cry. Alain met his attack with a parry and riposte, his sword piercing the man's heart with a

sickening thud. The man's lifeless body slumped to the ground, ending the brutal struggle.

Silence descended upon the clearing, broken only by the groans of the wounded and the mournful cries of the

Mi'kmaq. The air was thick with the scent of blood and woodsmoke. Casualties were heavy on both sides. One of the Mi'kmaq women, despite her bravery, had succumbed to her wounds. Her loss weighed heavily on the hearts of both the Templars and the remaining Mi'kmaq, a stark reminder of the fragility of life. Alain, his face grimy and streaked with blood, knelt beside her body, a silent prayer escaping his lips. He had seen death before, countless times on the battlefields of the Holy Land, but this felt different. This was not a clash of armies, but a brutal assault on a community that had offered them sanctuary.

The aftermath of the battle was a grim task. The dead were tended to, their bodies respectfully prepared. The wounded, both Templar and Mi'kmaq, were carefully cared for, their injuries tended to with herbs and meager supplies. The atmosphere was heavy with grief and exhaustion, but also with a newfound grim determination. The attack had been a brutal reminder of the dangers they faced, but it had also forged a deeper bond among the survivors, a sense of shared purpose that strengthened their resolve.

The question of who orchestrated the attack lingered. The attackers' weapons and tactics were crude, suggesting a band of opportunistic raiders, but their ferocity and knowledge of the encampment's layout hinted at a level of planning that implied something more. Was it a coincidence that the attack occurred so soon after their arrival? Had their presence been betrayed? The whispers of pursuit that had haunted them intensified, morphing into a tangible threat.

The discovery of a small, crudely drawn map amongst the dead offered a clue. It depicted the Templar encampment and showed a possible escape route leading towards the

coastline. A route that was also suspiciously close to a

known French fur-trading outpost. Could the French, ever

hungry for the Templar's legendary treasures, be behind this attack? Or perhaps it was a disgruntled native group, their resources depleted by the Templars' presence. The

possibilities were myriad, each one as chilling as the next.

As the survivors huddled around a meager fire, sharing what little food they had, the weight of their predicament bore down on them. The attack had shown them the fragility of their sanctuary. The whispers of pursuit were no longer faint murmurs; they were a deafening roar, the constant threat of discovery hanging over them like a dark cloud. Their journey was far from over; it had just become even more perilous. The serene beauty of the Nova Scotian wilderness was now shadowed by the ever-present danger. Their fight for survival, and the protection of their sacred treasures, was far from over. The attack was not simply a setback, but a bloody, brutal punctuation mark, underscoring the desperate stakes of their mission. The fight for survival had just begun anew, even more perilous than before. The harsh reality of their situation could not be ignored, yet it was the fierce hope borne of this shared peril that would push them

onwards. Their unlikely alliance, forged in the crucible of conflict, now represented not only survival, but the enduring resilience of the human spirit. The fight had only just begun.

Strengthening Defenses

The first rays of the weak winter sun cast long shadows across the snow-covered ground, illuminating the makeshift encampment. The previous night's attack had left its mark —a chilling reminder of their vulnerability. The air, sharp with the scent of pine and the lingering smell of woodsmoke, held a new tension. Brother Jean, his face grim but resolute, addressed the assembled Templars and Mi'kmaq.

"The wolves are at the door," he stated, his voice low but firm. "Their hunt will not cease. We cannot rely on luck or the kindness of the wilderness to protect us. We must build defenses that will repel any attack, defenses strong enough to withstand even the most determined assault."

The task before them was daunting. Their sanctuary, once a refuge, now felt exposed. The crude shelters, hastily constructed from branches and animal hides, offered little protection against determined attackers. The surrounding forest, once a source of solace, now felt like a suffocating cage, its dense undergrowth hiding potential enemies.

Alain, his scarred face reflecting the harsh reality of their situation, stepped forward. "We need more than sharpened sticks and prayer, Jean. We need walls, real walls. And we need them now." His words were practical, devoid of sentimentality, a reflection of the grim necessity of their situation.

The immediate priority was to reinforce the perimeter.

Working tirelessly, the Templars and Mi'kmaq felled trees, their axes ringing against the hard wood, a counterpoint to the hushed whispers of the forest. The fallen logs, stripped of their branches, formed a rudimentary palisade, a crude but effective barrier against any direct assault. The women, skilled in weaving and crafting, worked diligently, creating sturdy mats from reeds and grasses, using them to fill gaps between the logs and strengthen the makeshift walls.

The Mi'kmaq, intimately familiar with the terrain, guided the construction. They pointed out strategic locations for the palisade, ensuring it took advantage of natural obstacles, utilizing rocky outcrops and dense thickets to enhance its defensive capabilities. Their knowledge of the land was invaluable, transforming their vulnerability into a degree of strategic advantage. They also taught the Templars how to camouflage the palisade, blending it seamlessly into the surrounding landscape, minimizing its visibility from a distance.

Beyond the physical barriers, Jean stressed the importance of vigilance. He established a system of rotating guards, ensuring that watchful eyes scanned the perimeter day and night. The Templars, seasoned warriors, were adept at silent movement and keen observation. They were taught the art of silent patrol and how to detect signs of approaching enemies, such as broken twigs, disturbed snow, or the faintest scent of unfamiliar humans or animals.

The Mi'kmaq women contributed their unique skills, creating a network of warning signals using smoke and distinctive calls, echoing through the forest to alert the settlement of any potential danger. Their deep understanding of the natural world enabled them to create an early warning system,

effectively transforming the landscape itself into a watchful sentinel.

But physical defenses were only part of their strategy. Jean understood that their most valuable asset was their secrecy.

The very existence of their sanctuary had to remain unknown. To that end, they painstakingly cleared all traces of their encampment, meticulously eliminating any evidence of their presence. Footprints were covered, fires were extinguished without a trace, and waste was carefully disposed of, avoiding any indication of their numbers or routines. Stealth and concealment were to be their silent allies in this desperate struggle for survival.

The construction of traps was another crucial element of their improved defense. Alain, with his practical skills and his understanding of military engineering, took the lead. He taught the others how to create concealed pits lined with sharpened stakes, camouflaged with branches and snow. They also built tripwires, triggering noisy alarms to alert the defenders to an approaching enemy.

Their approach was not purely defensive. They understood the value of proactive measures. Regular patrols ventured into the surrounding forest, not only to scout for potential threats but also to lay traps and further enhance their security. These patrols served a dual purpose —reconnaissance and the reinforcement of the overall defensive perimeter. They were like silent tendrils, extending the reach of their defenses into the surrounding wilderness.

The nights were long and cold, filled with the crackling of the fire and the low murmurs of worried voices. However, the atmosphere within the encampment was far from despair.

The shared threat had forged a bond between the Templars and the Mi'kmaq, their initial hesitancy now replaced by a deep mutual respect and reliance. They worked side-by-side, sharing skills and knowledge, their combined efforts creating a fortress of survival in the heart of the harsh Nova Scotian winter.

The sense of community was palpable. Stories were shared, laughter intertwined with moments of anxious silence. The women sang haunting Mi'kmaq songs, their voices carrying on the wind, both a source of comfort and a poignant reminder of the fragility of their existence.

The work was backbreaking, but the progress was

undeniable. The improved defenses gradually instilled a sense of renewed confidence. Their makeshift sanctuary, once a precarious haven, was evolving into a formidable stronghold, a testament to their resilience and their unwavering determination to protect their sacred trust.

The attacks may continue, Jean knew. But the resolve of the defenders was now as hardened as the winter ground. The whispers of pursuit were still present, a constant reminder of the danger that loomed, but the sound was now tempered by the sound of axes felling trees, the clinking of tools, and the low hum of determined effort. The strength of their resolve was reflected in the improving defenses – a bulwark against the encroaching darkness. The fight for survival, far from being over, had entered a new, more determined phase, a testament to the enduring spirit of the Knights Templar and their newfound allies. The wilderness, once a silent observer, now bore witness to their struggle, and to the unwavering strength of the human spirit in the face of adversity. The fight was far from over, but for the first time, a flicker of hope ignited in the harsh reality of their circumstances. They were not simply surviving; they were fighting back. The future was still uncertain, shrouded in the cold embrace of the Nova Scotian winter, but the strength of their defenses, both physical and spiritual, offered a glimmer of hope in the encroaching darkness.

The Arrival of Inquisitors

The biting Nova Scotian wind whipped through the sparse trees, carrying with it not just the chill of the approaching winter, but a chilling whisper of impending doom. Brother Thomas, his face etched with worry lines deepened by the harsh climate and the weight of their secret, stood sentinel atop the rocky outcrop overlooking their makeshift settlement. For months, they had lived a precarious existence, their sanctuary hidden deep within the wilderness, a testament to their ingenuity and resilience. But the fragile peace was about to shatter.

A scout, his breath misting in the frigid air, hurried towards Thomas, his eyes wide with alarm. "Brother Thomas," he gasped, his voice barely audible above the wind's howl, "we've seen them. Inquisitors. Riding south from the settlements."

The news spread through the small community like wildfire. The whispers of the Inquisition, once a distant threat, had become a tangible, terrifying reality. The Papal decree, which had driven them from their homes in the Holy Land, had cast a long shadow across their lives, its chilling influence reaching even to this remote corner of the world. They had believed their sanctuary, their carefully concealed vault, would offer them protection. They had been wrong.

The men, hardened veterans of countless battles, felt a familiar chill crawl down their spines, a mixture of fear and grim determination. They had faced Saladin's armies, weathered the storms of the open sea, and endured the unforgiving wilderness. But the Inquisition... that was a different beast altogether. The Inquisition was not an army to be fought on a battlefield; it was a relentless, insidious force that could penetrate any defense, that hunted down its prey with the meticulous cruelty of a wolf stalking its quarry.

Brother Etienne, their leader, a man whose faith was as unwavering as the granite cliffs surrounding them, called a council. The flickering firelight cast long, dancing shadows on their grim faces as they gathered in their makeshift chapel, the air thick with a mixture of prayer and apprehension. The sacred relics, their burden and their salvation, were safe, for now. But their safety was inextricably linked to their own.

"We cannot stay here," Etienne declared, his voice firm despite the tremor of anxiety in his eyes. "The Inquisitors will find us. Their hounds are relentless. They will not rest until they have extinguished the last embers of the Templar Order."

The discussion that followed was fraught with tension. Some advocated for a defiant stand, a final battle against

overwhelming odds. Others, weary from years of flight and hardship, urged a retreat, a desperate flight into the deeper wilderness, seeking a new, more hidden sanctuary. The debate raged, the weight of their past, the urgency of their present, and the uncertainty of their future heavy upon them.

Days turned into a blur of frantic activity. They gathered supplies, prepared for a hasty departure. The meticulously crafted booby traps around their sanctuary, once a source of confidence, now seemed inadequate against the methodical and determined approach of the Inquisition. They were not simply soldiers; they were investigators, theologians, and torturers. Their methods were subtle, their reach extensive.

The decision was made. They would leave their carefully constructed haven, abandon the sanctuary they had built with such painstaking effort. It was a bitter pill to swallow, a testament to the unrelenting pressure of the Inquisition's relentless pursuit. But survival dictated that they must move, must fade back into the shadows, like phantoms in the wilderness. This was no longer a battle for territory; it was a fight for survival.

The escape was harrowing. The unforgiving terrain of Nova Scotia tested their physical and mental endurance. They moved silently, their every step measured, their senses alert to any sign of pursuit. The nights were long and filled with a constant undercurrent of anxiety, the fear of discovery a palpable presence. The days were little better, with the constant threat of ambush hanging over them like a shroud.

They travelled in small, dispersed groups, relying on their knowledge of the land and their skill in evasion to avoid detection. They moved under the cover of darkness, avoiding open areas, relying on the shadows and the dense forests for concealment. They were hunted, and they knew it. Every rustle of leaves, every snap of a twig, sent shivers of apprehension through their ranks. The Inquisitors were not just searching for them; they were hunting them, systematically and mercilessly.

They learned to live off the land, foraging for berries and roots, hunting small animals for sustenance. Their resources dwindled, their strength ebbed, but their determination remained unbroken. The spirit of the Templar Order, forged in the fires of adversity and persecution, burned brightly within them, guiding them through the darkness.

The knowledge of the Inquisitors' approach had given them a new perspective, a renewed sense of urgency. The years of

Exile had only strengthened the bonds of brotherhood among them. Each man knew he was not alone in his struggle; they were bound together by shared loss, shared faith and the shared burden of their sacred secret. This knowledge provided solace, inspiration, and renewed determination to evade their pursuers.

Their journey took them through dense forests, across treacherous rivers, and over unforgiving mountains. The landscape itself seemed to conspire against them, testing their resolve at every turn. The relentless pursuit never eased; the ever-present threat of discovery, the fear of torture and execution loomed constantly over them like a dark cloud.

One night, huddled around a meager fire, Brother Armand, a younger knight, spoke his fear openly, a break in the stoic silence that had become their constant companion. "Brother Etienne," he whispered, his voice heavy with despair, "will we ever escape this?"

Etienne placed a comforting hand on Armand's shoulder.

"We must escape, Armand," he replied, his voice firm, despite the weariness etched into his face. "For ourselves, yes, but also for the faith, for the Order, for the legacy we must protect. We are not merely escaping our pursuers; we are safeguarding the future."

His words offered a measure of comfort, a renewed sense of purpose. They knew their struggle was not merely a fight for survival; it was a sacred mission, a testament to their faith and to the enduring strength of the Templar spirit. The relentless pursuit of the Inquisition had only strengthened their resolve, fueled their determination to protect their secrets and ensure that the legacy of the Templars would survive. Their journey was far from over; the shadow of the

Inquisition still hung over them, but they pressed on, driven by hope, faith, and the unwavering conviction that their sacred mission must prevail.

Preparing for War

The sun, a weak, watery orb in the perpetually overcast sky, cast long shadows across the makeshift encampment.

Brother Thomas, his gaze still fixed on the distant horizon, descended the rocky outcrop, the crunch of dried leaves under his worn leather boots the only sound in the chilling silence. The relative peace of the past months had been a deceptive calm, a lull before the storm. The whispers of their pursuers, once faint murmurs on the wind, had grown into a tangible threat. The Inquisition, driven by a fanatical zeal and fueled by rumors of their hidden treasures, was closing in.

He found Brother Etienne, their master blacksmith, hunched over a forge, the flickering flames reflecting in his intense eyes. The air hung thick with the scent of coal smoke and hot metal. Etienne, a man whose strength belied his wiry frame, was meticulously sharpening a collection of swords and axes, their once-gleaming surfaces now dulled by months of hard use in the unforgiving wilderness.

"Brother Etienne," Thomas began, his voice low and gravelly from the cold, "how far are we from being fully prepared?"

Etienne straightened, wiping a smudge of soot from his cheek with the back of his hand. "We've made good

progress, Brother Thomas. The defenses around the

sanctuary are stronger than ever. The booby traps are all set, the tunnels reinforced, but... it's not enough. A full-scale assault... we'll need more."

Thomas nodded, his expression grim. "More than just fortifications. We need to consider every possibility. Food, water, weapons... even medical supplies. Winter is coming, and with it, an even greater challenge. They will be relentless."

The preparations began immediately. Brother Guillaume, a former Templar physician, meticulously checked their meager supply of herbs and remedies, his brow furrowed in concern. The harsh conditions had taken their toll on their health, and even a minor injury could prove fatal in their isolated sanctuary. He carefully sorted through the few remaining bandages, sighing at the limited quantity. He knew that they would need far more if a full-scale attack resulted in injuries.

Brother Jean-Luc, a master woodsman, oversaw the gathering of firewood. The forest, once a source of abundance, was now showing signs of depletion, each felled tree a visible reminder of their dwindling resources. He knew they needed to supplement their wood supply with other materials for warmth and cooking during the harsh Nova Scotian winters. They needed to gather peat and other resources that would be less difficult to obtain during the winter months. He meticulously stacked the logs, ensuring that they would last through the coming months, his efforts reflecting the seriousness of the impending winter. He also began planning strategic locations for firewood gathering to make future acquisitions easier and quicker, so that they didn't lose precious time in case of an attack.

Brother Geoffroy, a skilled hunter and tracker, led a small party deep into the forest in search of game. The animals, wary and scarce after months of relentless hunting, were becoming increasingly elusive. Geoffroy, however, possessed an almost supernatural ability to read the tracks and signs of the forest, his keen eyes spotting the slightest disturbance in the undergrowth. He understood the importance of supplementing their diminishing food

resources, not just with meat from hunting but also with foraging for edible plants and berries. He knew that their survival might depend on his ability to provide sustenance during the lean winter months. He led his team methodically, carefully assessing the surrounding area for traps and danger.

He explained his hunting and tracking strategies to the younger brothers, ensuring they developed the necessary skills for long-term survival.

Meanwhile, Brother Armand, a former Templar architect, oversaw the fortification of the sanctuary itself. He directed the brothers in strengthening the wooden palisades, reinforcing the earthworks, and setting additional traps along the approaches. He meticulously inspected each section of the wall, ensuring that it could withstand a prolonged siege.

He understood that the sanctuary was not just a place of refuge, but a symbol of their continued resistance. The brothers worked tirelessly, their movements synchronized and efficient, a testament to years of military training and their unwavering resolve. Their efforts were not only about physical defenses; they were about reinforcing their unity and strengthening their spirits to face the coming conflict.

He even created concealed escape routes, in case the sanctuary was overrun.

Days bled into weeks, each sunrise bringing the stark

realization of their precarious situation. The brothers worked tirelessly, their bodies aching, their spirits tested, but their determination unwavering. They hoarded every ounce of food, every drop of water, every piece of wood. They sharpened their weapons, honed their skills, and prepared themselves for a fight to the death. Their once-sacred mission of preserving their relics had expanded to encompass a fight for their very survival.

One evening, huddled around a meager fire, Thomas addressed the assembled brothers. "The time for stealth is over," he declared, his voice ringing with a newfound

resolve. "The Inquisition knows we are here. They will come for us. Let us meet them not with fear, but with unwavering faith and the strength of our convictions. We are Templars, and we will not yield."

A murmur of agreement rippled through the assembled brothers. Their faces, etched with exhaustion and worry, held a resolute glint. They had faced death many times before.

They had witnessed the horrors of war, the ruthlessness of their enemies, and the betrayal of those they once trusted.

But through it all, their faith and their brotherhood had remained steadfast.

The weight of history, the burden of their secret, and the relentless pressure of their pursuers had forged them into something stronger, more resilient. They were no longer just remnants of a fallen order. They were survivors, warriors, guardians of a legacy that refused to die. They were prepared to face the Inquisition, not just to defend their sanctuary but to defend their faith, their brotherhood, and their very right to exist. The coming conflict would be a test of their strength, their faith, and their unwavering belief in their cause, a test they were determined to pass with the courage and determination of true Templars. The very air crackled with the anticipation of their coming battle, a chilling

symphony of fear and determination echoing through their makeshift haven in the heart of the unforgiving Nova Scotian wilderness. Their prayers, their hopes, and their weapons were all they had. And they would fight for every inch of their hard-won sanctuary.

The preparations continued throughout the night, a silent ballet of determined men working in the darkness. They sharpened their weapons, checked their armor, and

reinforced their fortifications. They prayed for guidance, for strength, and for the protection of God. The silence was punctuated only by the crackling fire, the rustling leaves, and the occasional whispered prayer. They knew the dawn would bring not only the light of a new day, but also the shadow of the Inquisition, the shadow of a relentless enemy who sought to extinguish their faith and erase their history. But they were ready. They were Templars. And they would fight. They had lived a precarious existence, but they would not be easily defeated. They had learned the art of survival; they would now demonstrate the art of warfare. The preparation was not just about physical strength, but about spiritual resilience, a final communion of brothers before the imminent battle.

The air hung heavy with the foreboding of the coming storm, a chilling blend of anticipation and dread. The chilling wind whispered through the trees, carrying the silent promise of a confrontation that would determine their fate. The brothers knew they were outnumbered, outgunned, and perhaps outmatched. But they were united, and their faith was unwavering. They stood poised on the edge of a precipice, ready to face the storm, to defend their sanctuary, and to safeguard their precious legacy. They were ready to fight for their lives, for their faith, for their brotherhood, and for the future of the Knights Templar. The shadow of the Inquisition loomed, but the light of their unwavering faith burned

brightly within their hearts. And it was that light, that faith, that would guide them through the darkness that lay ahead. The dawn brought with it not just light but a palpable sense of impending conflict.

Strategic Retreat

The decision hung heavy in the crisp morning air, a tangible weight pressing down on the shoulders of the remaining Knights Templar. Brother Thomas, his face etched with the lines of sleepless nights and the burden of leadership, addressed the small gathering huddled around a meager fire. The flames danced and flickered, casting flickering shadows that mimicked the uncertainty twisting within their hearts.

"Brothers," he began, his voice low and gravelly, each word carrying the weight of centuries of history and the gravity of their current predicament. "The whispers have become shouts. The shadow of the Inquisition is no longer a looming threat, but a tangible presence, closing in like a predator upon its prey. Our sanctuary, once a haven of peace and refuge, is now a beacon, drawing the hunters closer."

A murmur rippled through the assembled knights. Their faces, hardened by years of war and hardship, reflected a mixture of grim acceptance and reluctant resignation.

Brother Guillaume, his usually boisterous spirit subdued, spoke up. "We have held this place for many months,

Brother Thomas. We have fortified it, concealed our relics, and fought off attacks. But this feels different. The

Inquisition's resources are far greater than those of any other threat we've faced. We are outnumbered, outmatched, and running out of time."

Brother Etienne, a younger knight but fierce in his devotion, nodded in agreement. "They will not rest until they find us and seize what they believe we hold. Their greed knows no bounds, and their faith in their own righteousness makes them ruthless and unstoppable." His eyes hardened with a barely concealed rage. He'd witnessed firsthand the barbarity of the Inquisition's methods, the relentless zeal that fueled their hunts, and the agonizing deaths they inflicted upon those they deemed heretics.

The silence that followed was heavy, broken only by the crackle of the dying fire and the mournful cry of a hawk circling overhead. The decision, though unspoken, was palpable. Their current position, once a sanctuary, was now a death trap. A strategic retreat, a move to a location unknown even to themselves, was their only hope of survival.

Thomas continued, his voice gaining strength, drawing upon the unwavering faith that had sustained them through years of adversity. "We cannot remain here. To stay is to invite annihilation. We must retreat, but this retreat will not be a flight. It will be a strategic repositioning, a calculated move to buy us time, to allow us to safeguard our sacred trust and ensure the continuation of our order."

The plan, painstakingly crafted over the preceding weeks based on fragmented maps and cryptic clues left by previous generations of Knights Templar, involved a perilous journey through the treacherous Nova Scotian wilderness. Their destination: a hidden valley nestled deep within the rugged landscape, a place known only to a select few, shrouded in myth and legend.

The logistical preparations were meticulous and demanding. Each knight had a specific role in the evacuation. Brother Jean-Luc, a master of disguise and infiltration, was tasked with leading the reconnaissance mission, scouting the route ahead for potential dangers and identifying any signs of Inquisitorial pursuit. His eyes, keen and observant, were legendary, and his ability to blend into the shadows unparalleled.

Brother Marc, a skilled cartographer and navigator,

meticulously prepared their route, charting their course through dense forests, across treacherous rivers, and over unforgiving mountains. He possessed an innate sense of direction, his knowledge of the wilderness unparalleled. His maps were more than just drawings; they were keys to survival.

The task of concealing and transporting the sacred relics was entrusted to Brother Armand, a man of immense strength and unwavering loyalty. The artifacts, concealed within specially crafted containers, were cleverly disguised amongst their mundane provisions. His role was not just physical; he was also the protector of their sacred legacy.

The evacuation itself was a delicate dance of secrecy and speed. Under the cover of darkness, the Knights Templar silently dismantled their camp, meticulously erasing all traces of their presence. They moved with the efficiency and precision honed from years of military training, their

movements silent and coordinated.

Their journey was arduous, filled with peril and hardship.

They navigated through treacherous terrain, their bodies battered and bruised, their spirits tested by exhaustion and uncertainty. The constant threat of discovery loomed over them, a shadow that never completely vanished. They encountered hostile wildlife, the unforgiving climate, and the ever-present fear of the Inquisitorial pursuit.

Brother Jean-Luc, leading the scouting party, regularly returned with reports of unsettling discoveries. The

Inquisition's tracks, though faint, were undeniable,

suggesting they were closing in from multiple directions. They had to maintain a constant vigilance, always looking over their shoulder, always prepared to react to the sudden appearance of their relentless foes. The Knights' resilience and faith were relentlessly tested, and some began to doubt their prospects.

One particularly harrowing incident involved their crossing of a raging river. A sudden storm transformed the already dangerous rapids into a churning torrent. Their small raft was tossed about like a leaf in a hurricane, threatening to capsize and send them to their watery graves. It was a display of combined strength and teamwork that saw them make it to the other side, battered but alive.

Days turned into weeks, and the relentless pressure of the chase pushed the Knights to their physical and emotional limits. The shortage of food and water, the ever-present danger of discovery, and the psychological strain of constant fear began to take its toll. Brother Guillaume, once the strongest and most jovial of the group, began to exhibit signs of despair and doubt.

However, Brother Thomas, with his unwavering faith and steely resolve, continuously reminded them of their purpose. He recounted stories of their Order's resilience, emphasizing the importance of their mission and the significance of their sacred trust. His words, filled with faith and hope, helped bolster the spirits of his brothers and keep them going. He reminded them of the generations of Templars who had sacrificed everything to protect their faith and the sacred relics they carried, echoing through the ages.

Finally, after weeks of relentless travel, exhaustion, and peril, the Knights Templar reached their destination: a hidden valley, shrouded in mist and silence. The valley, secluded and protected by towering cliffs and dense forest, was indeed a sanctuary, a refuge from the relentless pursuit of the Inquisition.

The sense of relief was palpable, but it was mingled with a profound awareness that their struggle was far from over. The Inquisition's grasp would likely not relinquish so easily. Their newfound sanctuary wouldn't be a permanent respite, but merely a strategic foothold in their ongoing struggle for survival. Their fight was not merely for their own lives, but for the preservation of their sacred legacy, a legacy that extended far beyond their immediate existence, a beacon of hope in the face of overwhelming darkness. The journey had been harrowing, fraught with danger and uncertainty, but it had forged their brotherhood even stronger, a testament to their faith and endurance. And as they looked out upon the silent, protected valley, they knew that their fight for survival was far from over. They had a new sanctuary, a new beginning, but the shadows of the Inquisition still loomed, and the fight for their future was far from won.

A Desperate Flight

The wind howled a mournful dirge through the skeletal branches of the ancient pines, mirroring the turmoil in Brother Thomas's heart. Their sanctuary, a hidden valley nestled deep within the Nova Scotian wilderness, offered a deceptive sense of peace. The reality was a constant, gnawing anxiety – the shadow of the Inquisition stretched long and dark, threatening to engulf them at any moment. They were safe, for now, but the knowledge that the hounds of the Church were undoubtedly on their trail fueled a restless energy within their ranks.

Their escape from the Holy Land had been a desperate flight, a harrowing race against time and the relentless pursuit of their enemies. The memories were still raw, etched into their minds like scars. The betrayal in Acre, the panicked scramble to secure the sacred relics, the blood-chilling screams of their brothers betrayed and slaughtered in the night... the images haunted their dreams, fueling their determination to survive.

They had traveled light, discarding all but the most essential supplies and, of course, the sacred artifacts – the chalice, the cross, the ancient scrolls – entrusted to their care. Each item represented a piece of their history, a testament to their faith, and their very survival depended on their safekeeping. The weight of this responsibility was a heavy burden, shared equally amongst the remaining brothers.

Their journey had been a relentless test of endurance. Days bled into weeks, marked by the relentless pounding of their feet on the unforgiving terrain, the gnawing hunger that clawed at their bellies, the chilling winds that whipped through their meager clothing. They navigated treacherous mountain passes, forded icy rivers, and evaded the watchful eyes of hostile natives, their distrust a formidable barrier alongside the threat of the Inquisition.

Brother Etienne, ever the pragmatist, had devised a route that avoided main trails and settlements, relying on his intimate knowledge of the wilderness gleaned from years spent exploring the regions around the Holy Land. His skills in navigation and survival were invaluable. Yet, even with his expertise, the danger remained palpable. The dense forests concealed both protection and peril, offering a sanctuary from the direct gaze of their pursuers but also creating a realm of its own challenges, of unseen predators and the ever-present threat of getting lost, never to be found.

One night, huddled around a meager fire beneath the canopy of stars, Brother Geoffrey, the youngest of their number, confessed his fear. The ordeal had taken its toll on him, the constant fear and hardship revealing a vulnerability he had tried to hide. His fear, however, was not selfish; it was born from a deep concern for the others.

Brother Thomas, placing a comforting hand on the young knight's shoulder, spoke with quiet resolve. "Fear is a natural response, Geoffrey," he said, his voice low and steady, "but it should not paralyze us. We have faced worse, and we have overcome it. Our faith, our brotherhood – these are our

strengths. Let us not allow fear to erode them."

His words were a balm to the younger knight's soul. The shared experience had indeed forged an unbreakable bond between them. Their collective strength, forged in the crucible of adversity, fueled their relentless progress. They were more than just knights; they were a family, bound together by a shared purpose, a sacred trust, and the unshakeable belief in their cause.

The constant threat of discovery kept them on edge. Every rustle in the undergrowth, every snap of a twig, sent a jolt of adrenaline through them. They slept lightly, their senses perpetually heightened, their weapons close at hand. The memories of their brethren, cruelly murdered for their faith, served as a stark reminder of the stakes.

Brother Jean-Luc, their healer and a man of deep faith, maintained their spirits with his unwavering optimism and quiet strength. His knowledge of herbal remedies proved invaluable, easing the pain of their wounds and soothing their aching muscles. His prayers, offered under the vast expanse of the night sky, offered comfort and solace in the face of their overwhelming challenges.

The terrain grew more challenging as they pressed deeper into the wilderness. Bogs threatened to swallow them whole, steep ravines tested their nerve, and thickets of thorny bushes tore at their clothing. They relied on each other, their combined skills and strengths forming an unbreakable chain. Brother Armand, a veteran of countless battles, expertly set traps and patrols, using his considerable knowledge to protect them from both human and animal threats.

One terrifying encounter involved a pack of wolves, drawn by the scent of their dwindling supplies. The night was filled with the terrifying howls of the predators, their shadows stalking them through the darkness. The knights fought back valiantly, their swords flashing in the moonlight, their courage tempered by the desperation of the situation. They emerged victorious but wounded, their hearts pounding in their chests, a sobering reminder of the constant dangers that lurked in their path.

Days turned into weeks, weeks into months. The relentless pursuit seemed to stretch into eternity, a chilling reminder of the formidable force they were running from. Yet, amidst the hardship and the fear, their faith remained unwavering. The shared burden of their quest bound them together, each brother relying on the strength and resilience of the other.

Their journey was not merely a physical one; it was a spiritual pilgrimage, a test of faith and fortitude. They endured not only the harsh realities of the wilderness but also the gnawing doubts and fears that threatened to consume them. The weight of their past, the uncertainty of their future, the constant threat of capture – these were invisible foes, as dangerous as any they had faced with blade and shield.

But their belief in their sacred mission sustained them. The preservation of the relics, the safeguarding of their legacy –these were the beacons that guided their steps, lighting their path through the deepest darkness. The memory of their fallen brothers served as a constant reminder of the price of failure.

As they approached their destination, a sense of anticipation mixed with apprehension filled them. The valley, their haven, lay ahead, promising respite but offering no guarantee of lasting safety. The shadow of the Inquisition still loomed, a constant reminder that their flight was not yet over. Their struggle for survival was far from won, but in their unwavering brotherhood and their unyielding faith, they found the strength to carry on, ready to face whatever challenges lay ahead. Their journey had just begun.

Seeking Refuge

The valley opened before them like a welcoming, if slightly ominous, embrace. Towering pines, their needles a deep, almost black green against the fading light, formed a natural amphitheater around a small, crystal-clear lake. A waterfall cascaded down a rocky cliff face, its roar a constant, almost deafening soundtrack to their arrival. The air, thick with the scent of pine and damp earth, was a stark contrast to the salty tang of the sea they had left behind. Brother Thomas, his face etched with the weariness of their arduous journey, dismounted his weary horse, a sigh escaping his lips.

"This will do," he announced, his voice hoarse but firm, the words carrying a weight of both relief and apprehension. He looked at his brethren, their faces a mixture of exhaustion and cautious optimism. Sir Geoffrey, ever the pragmatist, immediately began assessing their surroundings. He examined the terrain, his gaze sharp and calculating. Brother Etienne, the youngest of their number, his youthful

exuberance tempered by the gravity of their situation, moved to tend to the horses, his hands gentle but efficient. Even Brother Giles, the aged scribe, whose frail body had borne the brunt of the journey, found a spark of renewed energy in the promise of temporary safety.

Their haven was far from perfect. The valley, while

secluded, offered limited defensible positions. The sheer cliffs provided some protection, but any sustained siege would be difficult to withstand. Their immediate priority was to establish a secure perimeter and construct temporary shelters. They worked with a quiet efficiency, the years of military discipline honed to a fine edge by the constant threat of pursuit. Sir Geoffrey, with his innate leadership, directed the efforts, his commands clear and concise. Brother Etienne, despite his youth, proved surprisingly adept at gathering firewood and preparing a meager meal. Brother Giles, though weakened, meticulously cataloged their remaining supplies.

As darkness descended, casting long, eerie shadows across the valley, a fire crackled merrily in the center of their makeshift camp. The flames danced and flickered, casting a warm glow on the weathered faces of the Knights. The crackling fire was a beacon of hope in the gathering gloom, a symbol of their resilience and unwavering faith. Around the fire, they shared what little food they had left – hardtack biscuits and dried meats, a stark reminder of their meager provisions. The silence, broken only by the crackling fire and the distant howl of a wolf, was pregnant with unspoken anxieties.

The conversation, though subdued, was far from idle. Their escape from the Holy Land had been harrowing, a near-constant flight from the clutches of the Inquisition. The decree of Pope Clement V, condemning the Knights Templar to death, had sent shockwaves through their ranks. The betrayal by those they had served faithfully for so long had left a deep wound, a festering sore that would take time to heal. They had been forced to abandon their grand preceptory in Jerusalem, leaving behind not just their homes but also their comrades, many of whom had already met gruesome fates at the hands of their persecutors.

The escape itself had been a miracle, a carefully orchestrated maneuver that involved subterfuge, cunning, and a dash of sheer luck. The transport of the sacred relics, the most significant of which were secretly concealed amongst their personal belongings, had demanded equal measures of skill and bravery, with many daring escapes narrowly avoiding

capture. They had slipped through the fingers of their
pursuers, utilizing a network of loyal contacts and hidden routes.
The journey across the seas to the harsh and
unforgiving wilderness of Nova Scotia had been brutal, a test of
their physical and mental endurance.

Now, nestled in their temporary sanctuary, they faced the daunting
task of planning their next move. They were safe for the moment, but
their flight was far from over. The Inquisition's long arm stretched far
and wide, its influence extending even into the remote corners of the
world. The very existence of the Knights Templar was now a treasonous
act, punishable by the most brutal methods the church could muster.
They were fugitives, hunted men, their lives hanging by a thread.

Brother Thomas, gazing into the flames, spoke, his voice heavy with
the weight of their shared burden. "We must decide on our course of
action," he declared. "We cannot remain here indefinitely. This valley
provides only
temporary respite. Our true sanctuary lies elsewhere, a place where
we can lay down our burdens and ensure the survival of the Order."

Sir Geoffrey nodded gravely. "I agree. We need to secure a more
permanent hiding place – one that will not only shield us from our
immediate pursuers but also safeguard the relics entrusted to our care."
He then spoke of a possible location they had heard rumors of before
leaving the Holy Land - a secluded and ancient settlement, far away and
lost within the thickest and deepest forest of Nova Scotia, where they
would be able to not only protect themselves but secure their sacred
artifacts, from the reach of the Inquisitors.

Brother Etienne, eager to contribute, suggested that they should
also consider establishing contact with potential allies

– those who sympathized with their cause and might offer assistance. The task would be perilous, but the potential rewards outweighed the risks. There were those who still believed in the Order and their purpose. Finding those faithful souls would be crucial to their survival.

Brother Giles, ever the voice of reason, cautioned against rash actions. "We must proceed with caution," he warned. "Any contact with the outside world carries inherent risks. A single indiscretion could expose our position and undo all our efforts." His words were wise, a sobering reminder of the fragility of their situation.

Their discussion continued long into the night, fueled by the warmth of the fire and the strength of their brotherhood.

They debated the merits of various options, weighing the risks and rewards of each course of action. They

meticulously planned their next steps, utilizing their

combined knowledge and experience to formulate a strategy that would maximize their chances of survival. They discussed how to evade detection, create defensive barriers, and stockpile supplies. They even created a series of coded messages that could be used to communicate with sympathetic allies, should they ever find any.

As dawn broke, casting a soft, ethereal light across the valley, a sense of purpose replaced the previous anxiety. They were not merely survivors; they were protectors of a sacred legacy, guardians of a faith that had been unjustly persecuted. They were the last embers of a dying flame, determined to keep the light of their Order alive, no matter the cost. They had found refuge for now, but their journey was far from over. The shadow of the Inquisition still loomed large, but they were ready to face whatever challenges lay ahead. Their courage, their faith, and their brotherhood would be their shields against the darkness, guiding them on their perilous path toward a future that remained uncertain, yet full of a fierce hope for survival.

Their fate was far from sealed, as they prepared to face the treacherous path ahead, carrying within them a resolute spirit that would not easily be extinguished.

Finding a New Hiding Place

The Nova Scotian winter had tested their resilience, pushing them to the brink of despair. The relentless storms, the biting cold that seeped into their bones, the constant struggle for food – it had chipped away at their strength, both physical and spiritual. But the icy grip of the wilderness had not broken their resolve. Their sacred mission, the preservation of the relics entrusted to them, remained their unwavering purpose. The temporary sanctuary they'd established had served its purpose, offering respite from immediate pursuit, but it was not a permanent solution. The whispers of the Inquisition, carried on the wind, still haunted them. They needed a new hiding place, a sanctuary more secure, more impenetrable.

Their search began in the aftermath of the retreat. Sir

Geoffroi, their leader, a man hardened by years of combat but now bearing the weight of their collective burden,

surveyed the landscape with a weary eye. The forest, once a refuge, now seemed to press in on them, its dark shadows concealing potential dangers. Their escape had been harrowing, a desperate flight through unforgiving terrain, and the lingering exhaustion weighed heavily upon them. Each man carried the scars of their flight – physical wounds, frostbite, and the deeper wounds inflicted by the betrayal they still suspected lurked amongst them.

They moved slowly, cautiously, their senses heightened, alert for any sign of pursuit. They traveled light, carrying only the bare necessities, rationing their dwindling supplies. The precious relics remained hidden, secured in a makeshift container, their weight a constant reminder of the responsibility they bore. The landscape had shifted, the terrain becoming more mountainous, the forests denser and darker. They were moving further inland, away from the coastal settlements, seeking a place where they could disappear, where the very earth would protect them from the eyes of their enemies.

Days bled into weeks. The relentless search was a grueling test of endurance. They relied on their shared knowledge of survival techniques, honed during years spent on campaign, but even that seemed insufficient against the harshness of the wild Nova Scotian landscape. They encountered wildlife –deer, wolves, and the occasional bear – a constant reminder of the dangers that lurked beyond the threat of human

enemies. They hunted, fished, and foraged, their skills sharpening with necessity. They learned to trust their instincts, to read the subtle signs of the land.

One evening, huddled around a meager fire, Brother Thomas, a scholar amongst the Knights, spoke of the legends of the region. Tales of hidden caves, of ancient passages lost to time. He spoke of a place known only to the local Mi'kmaq people, a network of caverns hidden deep within the mountains, a place said to be impregnable. This sparked a renewed hope, a glimmer of light in the encroaching darkness of despair. The legend offered a potential solution, a possible new sanctuary.

Following the faint clues gleaned from Brother Thomas's research, supplemented by their tentative communication with the Mi'kmaq, they set off once more. This time, their journey was different; it was fueled not by the desperation of flight but by a newfound purpose. The arduous climb was hampered by the deep snowdrifts and the freezing temperatures. The relentless wind howled through the barren mountains like the cries of the damned. Yet, they persevered, driven by a faith that had been strengthened by adversity, spurred by the hope of finding a refuge to shield their sacred trust from the reach of their pursuers.

The days were punctuated by moments of agonizing doubt and moments of fragile hope. They pushed onward, their resolve unwavering, each step an act of defiance against the odds stacked against them. Their journey led them through canyons carved by ancient glaciers and across treacherous ravines, through blizzards that threatened to bury them alive.

They relied on each other, sharing their burdens, sharing their fears, and sharing their unwavering faith. Their journey was a testament to their brotherhood, a living embodiment of the bonds forged in the fires of adversity.

Finally, after what seemed like an eternity, they found it. A narrow fissure in a cliff face, almost imperceptible against the stark backdrop of the mountain. It was a hidden entrance to a network of caves, a labyrinthine system that extended deep into the earth. The air within was damp and cold, carrying the scent of earth and stone, but it was protected from the wind and the snow. It was a place of darkness and mystery, but it was also a place of potential refuge.

The entrance was narrow, barely wide enough to allow a single man to pass. It was almost completely concealed, hidden behind a curtain of ice, blending seamlessly into the frozen landscape. The first few meters were cramped and difficult to navigate, requiring them to crawl and squeeze through narrow passages. But as they ventured deeper, the caverns opened up, revealing vast chambers and winding tunnels.

The task of relocating the relics was daunting. The passages were treacherous, dark, and difficult to navigate. The risk of injury, or even death, was ever-present. They worked

tirelessly, slowly and cautiously, each man performing his task with meticulous care. They secured the relics within a secluded chamber, far from the main entrance, a place where they would be hidden from prying eyes. They reinforced the walls, creating a secure vault within the already hidden chamber. They used natural materials – stone, wood, and earth – to construct the vault, camouflaging it within the natural formations of the cavern.

The effort was monumental, requiring days of backbreaking labor. The physical strain was immense, but their resolve remained unshaken. They worked in shifts, sharing the burden, keeping each other's spirits up with prayers and songs. The darkness, the cold, and the constant physical demands threatened to overwhelm them, but the thought of preserving their sacred trust fueled their tireless efforts. Their combined knowledge of engineering and construction allowed them to devise ingenious mechanisms to secure the entrance, ensuring that their hidden sanctuary would remain undiscovered.

Once the relics were safely secured, the Knights began the arduous task of making the new cavern a livable space. They collected firewood, carefully choosing dry branches and logs, avoiding the dampness that permeated the lower levels of the cavern system. They built a makeshift fire pit and fashioned beds using salvaged materials and animal skins, creating a small, but habitable space in the heart of their subterranean refuge.

The air within the cavern was damp and cold, a stark

contrast to the harsh winter outside, but it offered a level of protection that they had not experienced before. The

darkness was absolute, broken only by the flickering light of their small fire. But the darkness, paradoxically, became their ally, hiding them from the prying eyes of their enemies.

It was a new beginning, a new chapter in their long and

arduous journey. The search for a new sanctuary had been successful; they had found a place where they could finally rest, where they could regroup, and where they could plan their next move. The weight of their past, however, continued to weigh heavily upon them, a constant reminder of the challenges that still lay ahead. The journey was far from over, but for now, at least, they were safe. They were hidden. They were, for the moment, secure.

Adapting to a New Environment

The damp chill of the cavern clung to them like a shroud, a constant reminder of their precarious situation. Brother Thomas, his face etched with the weariness of countless sleepless nights, stoked the meager fire, its flickering flames casting dancing shadows on the rough-hewn walls. The air, thick with the smell of woodsmoke and damp earth, was far from pleasant, but it offered a respite from the biting wind that howled outside. Their new sanctuary, a hidden cavern nestled deep within a seemingly impenetrable cliff face, was far from luxurious, but it offered a level of security they hadn't known since their escape from the Holy Land.

The initial euphoria of finding refuge quickly gave way to the practicalities of survival. They were a band of men accustomed to the comforts – relative comforts – of the Templar order, not to the harsh realities of a wilderness existence. The transition was jarring. Their skills, honed in the heat of battle, were of little use in this new environment. Hunting, foraging, and shelter construction were skills they had to relearn, skills they had to hone with a desperate urgency.

Brother Etienne, a man of surprising resourcefulness, took the lead in establishing their new camp. He possessed a practical knowledge of the land, gleaned from studying maps and historical accounts during their years in the Holy Land.

He knew how to identify edible plants, how to set traps for small game, and how to create rudimentary tools from the materials at hand. Under his guidance, they fashioned makeshift beds from branches and furs scavenged from fallen animals. They constructed a rudimentary water collection system, channeling rainwater into a clay pot.

The challenge of adapting to the environment was immense. The winter clung stubbornly to the land, its icy grip refusing to release. They battled frostbite, hunger, and the ever-present threat of illness. The scarcity of food was a constant worry. Their hunting attempts were often fruitless, and the meager supply of dried provisions they had brought with them dwindled at an alarming rate. Brother Geoffroi, a man of immense strength and unwavering faith, bore the brunt of the hunting efforts, his perseverance almost super-human in its intensity.

The physical hardships were compounded by the

psychological burden of their situation. The constant fear of discovery, the weight of their past, the uncertainty of their future – these were burdens that weighed heavily on their minds. Brother Guillaume, a man known for his wisdom and calming presence, became their spiritual anchor. His quiet faith and unwavering belief in divine providence proved a source of strength for the group. Every night, he led them in prayer, his voice a soothing balm in the chilling darkness of their cave. The prayers, a familiar ritual from their life in the Holy Land, provided a comforting sense of continuity in the midst of chaos.

Their isolation was not total, however. Their new home, while hidden, was not inaccessible. They discovered a

narrow passage, almost invisible from the outside, that led to a small, hidden spring. It provided them with fresh, clean water, and it also served as a secret point of contact with the outside world. One day, while Brother Jean was fetching water, he noticed tracks—not animal tracks, but human tracks. The implications were chilling. Were they being followed? Were their enemies closer than they thought?

The discovery sparked a debate amongst the brothers. The relative security of their new haven was now threatened. Some argued for immediate relocation, fearing the potential danger that lurked outside. Others suggested strengthening their defenses, setting traps, and making their hidden entrance even more secure. Brother Armand, always pragmatic and thoughtful, suggested a reconnaissance mission. He proposed that a few of them venture out to investigate the tracks, assess the threat, and gather information before taking any decisive action.

The reconnaissance mission proved treacherous. They ventured out under the cover of darkness, their senses heightened, their weapons at the ready. The forest was a maze of shadow and sound. Every rustle of leaves, every snap of a twig, sent shivers down their spines. They followed the trail of human tracks, their hearts pounding in their chests. They discovered evidence of a small encampment – a makeshift camp, crudely constructed, but unmistakably human. The evidence suggested that their pursuers were not far behind.

The discovery confirmed their worst fears. Their enemies were close, their pursuit relentless. This newfound knowledge forced a change in strategy. The peaceful assimilation into their new home was over. Their focus shifted from mere survival to defense, from passive adaptation to active resistance.

The brothers set about strengthening their defenses. They concealed their entrance even further, using branches and vegetation to camouflage it. They laid booby traps and sharpened sharpened stakes around their perimeter. Brother Etienne's knowledge of local plants proved invaluable. He created a potent mixture of herbs and berries that acted as a repellent against animals and humans alike. They spent days

refining and improving their defensive measures,
transforming their hidden cavern into a formidable fortress.

Despite the daunting reality of their predicament, a quiet determination settled over the brothers. They were Knights Templar, sworn to defend the faith and protect the sacred relics entrusted to their care. Their plight was not just a struggle for survival; it was a fight for the legacy of their order, a battle against those who sought to extinguish the light of their faith. Their resilience, forged in the crucible of adversity, emerged as their greatest weapon. The wilderness, once a daunting adversary, had become their teacher. Their ability to adapt, to survive, and to protect their secrets had grown with every passing day, despite the ever-present

threat. They were alone, hunted, and far from home, but they were far from defeated. Their new sanctuary would hold, or they would find a new one; and this time, they would be prepared. The journey was far from over, but their determination remained unbroken. The fight to safeguard their sacred heritage had only just begun.

Maintaining Faith

The rhythmic crashing of waves against the rocky shore was a constant, almost hypnotic, backdrop to their existence.

Brother Etienne, his normally jovial face etched with

concern, knelt beside Brother Thomas, who was tending to a small, feverish boy, one of the younger novices who had made the arduous journey from the Holy Land. The boy, barely a man, coughed weakly, his breaths shallow and ragged. The meager supplies they had managed to salvage were dwindling, and sickness, a constant companion in their exile, threatened to erode their already fragile strength.

Maintaining their faith, however, was proving to be as difficult a task as finding food and shelter. The isolation, the constant fear of discovery, the gnawing uncertainty of their future – these were powerful forces that threatened to chip away at the bedrock of their Templar vows. Doubt, a subtle yet insidious enemy, crept into the hearts of even the most devout. The unwavering conviction that had sustained them through years of conflict and persecution began to waver under the weight of their present circumstances.

Brother Geoffroi, a seasoned Templar who had witnessed the horrors of the Inquisition firsthand, took it upon himself to bolster the morale of his brothers. He understood the insidious nature of despair; he had seen it consume men stronger than any of them. Each evening, after the meager meal and the tending of the sick, he would gather the brothers around the fire, his voice a low, comforting rumble in the echoing cavern. He spoke not of grand victories or glorious battles, but of simple truths, of the enduring power of faith, of the resilience of the human spirit.

He recounted stories of their order's history, tales of

unwavering courage and unshakeable loyalty, stories that spoke of a time when their faith was a beacon of hope in a world consumed by darkness. He spoke of the saints and martyrs, of their unwavering devotion to God in the face of unimaginable suffering. His words, though laced with

sorrow for the losses they had endured, were imbued with an unwavering optimism, a quiet confidence that resonated with his listeners. He reminded them that their faith was not merely a set of doctrines or rituals; it was a living, breathing force, a source of strength that could sustain them through the darkest of times.

One evening, Geoffroi recounted the legend of Saint Thomas Becket, the Archbishop of Canterbury, who had been martyred for his unwavering defense of the Church. He spoke of Becket's courage, his unwavering faith, and his willingness to sacrifice everything for what he believed in. The story resonated deeply with the brothers. They, too, had been forced to make sacrifices, to endure hardships beyond measure, all in the name of their faith.

"Our faith," Geoffroi declared, his voice echoing in the cavern, "is not merely a belief in God, but a testament to the power of the human spirit. It is the strength that allows us to persevere in the face of adversity, to overcome hardship, and to find hope even in the darkest of hours."

Brother Lucas, a young man whose faith had been shaken by the relentless persecution they had endured, spoke up. "But Brother Geoffroi," he said, his voice trembling slightly, "how can we maintain our faith when everything we have known and loved has been taken from us?"

Geoffroi smiled gently. "Our faith," he replied, "is not dependent on our circumstances. It is not defined by our possessions or our position in the world. It is a deep, abiding conviction, a connection to something greater than ourselves. It is the unwavering belief that even in the darkest night, the dawn will eventually break."

He then began to sing a hymn, a Gregorian chant that echoed through the cavern, its ancient melody filling the space with a sense of peace and serenity. The other brothers joined in, their voices blending together in a powerful testament to their shared faith. Their voices, initially hesitant, grew stronger, their hymn a prayer for strength, for solace, and for the preservation of their sacred legacy.

The singing continued for a long time, the brothers' voices intertwining, creating a wall of sound that echoed the strength of their faith and resolve. The cavern, once a symbol of their exile, transformed into a sacred space, a sanctuary where their faith was renewed, their spirits lifted, and their brotherhood reaffirmed.

Brother Jean, usually a man of few words, approached Geoffroi after the hymn concluded. "Your words, brother," he said, "have given me renewed hope. I feel...strengthened."

Geoffroi nodded, a knowing smile on his face. "The strength of our faith, Brother Jean, lies not in our achievements, but in our resilience. It is in our ability to endure, to remain steadfast in our convictions, even when the world around us crumbles."

The following days saw a renewed sense of purpose among the brothers. They worked together, sharing tasks, supporting each other, their actions a testament to their renewed faith and brotherhood. They established a schedule of daily prayers and reflections, a time for each brother to share his thoughts and feelings, to seek comfort and understanding from his companions. The young novice, whose sickness had cast a pall over their sanctuary, slowly began to recover, his recovery a testament to the healing power of faith, of community, and of the unwavering support of his brothers.

They also began to enhance the security of their cavern sanctuary. The entrance, already well-concealed, was further fortified with additional booby traps and hidden passages, reflecting their renewed resolve to protect their sacred relics and their own lives. The wilderness, once a source of fear and uncertainty, now held a certain charm. It presented challenges, yes, but it also offered sustenance and a sense of seclusion and peace.

The discovery of a nearby spring provided them with a clean and reliable source of water, reducing their reliance on the dwindling supply they had brought with them. They learned to utilize the resources of the surrounding area, foraging for edible plants and trapping small game. Their skills, honed through necessity, transformed the wilderness from a threatening adversary into a source of sustenance. This interdependence with the land fostered a deeper connection amongst them, strengthening their bond and their resilience.

Their faith wasn't merely a religious practice, it was a way of life, influencing every aspect of their existence, from their prayers and rituals to their daily chores and interactions. It was the glue that held their brotherhood together, the compass that guided their actions, and the beacon of hope that illuminated their path in the darkness. The journey ahead would undoubtedly remain difficult, but their faith, strengthened and renewed, was a powerful weapon in the arsenal of their survival. Their sanctuary wasn't merely a physical refuge, it was a haven where they could nourish their spirits, and bolster their resilience in the face of overwhelming odds. The fight for their sacred heritage was far from over, but they were prepared, their faith their greatest shield, their brotherhood their most formidable sword.

Unexpected Discovery

The relentless Atlantic wind howled a mournful dirge,
whipping Brother Thomas's brown habit around him as he surveyed the rugged coastline. Days bled into weeks since their arrival on this unforgiving shore, a land starkly different from the sun-drenched hills of the Holy Land. The relentless search for a suitable hiding place for the sacred relics weighed heavily on their minds. The small cove they'd initially settled in offered little in the way of lasting security.

Their meager defenses were easily breached, and the constant threat of discovery hung heavy in the salty air.

Brother Etienne, his gaze fixed on a jagged cliff face,
pointed a weathered finger. "Look, Thomas. See that fissure?
It seems... unusual."

Thomas squinted, his eyes following the line of the fissure, a dark gash slicing through the grey stone. It was barely perceptible, almost swallowed by the shadows playing across the rock face. He approached cautiously, the ground beneath his feet treacherous with loose shale and slick seaweed. The air grew colder as he drew closer, a damp chill emanating from the narrow opening. He knelt, his hand tracing the rough edges of the fissure, feeling a subtle tremor beneath his fingertips.

"It feels... hollow," he murmured, a sense of anticipation tightening in his chest.

Together, the two brothers began to clear away the debris obstructing the entrance. The task was arduous, requiring both strength and patience. They worked tirelessly, their determination fueled by the urgent need to secure their sacred burden. Hours passed, the sun sinking low in the sky, casting long shadows that stretched and danced across the landscape. As the last of the rubble was cleared, a low, dark opening revealed itself, hinting at a passage beyond.

Brother Etienne, armed with a makeshift torch fashioned from twisted branches and resin, ventured into the darkness.

The air within was thick with the scent of damp earth and something else, something ancient and indefinable. The passage was narrow and uneven, forcing them to proceed with caution. The sound of their own breathing and the occasional drip of water echoed eerily in the confined space.

The tunnel twisted and turned, descending gradually into the earth. The torchlight revealed rough-hewn walls, slick with moisture, their surfaces adorned with strange markings that seemed both ancient and alien. As they delved deeper, the air grew noticeably warmer, a stark contrast to the biting wind outside. The sound of water trickling became a steady

murmur, growing louder with every step.

After what seemed like an eternity, the passage opened into a vast cavern. The sight that greeted them was breathtaking. The cavern was immense, its ceiling lost in the shadows far above. A subterranean stream meandered through the center, its waters crystal clear, reflecting the flickering torchlight in a mesmerizing dance of light and shadow. The walls of the cavern were smooth, polished by the relentless passage of water over millennia. Strange formations of rock, sculpted by time and nature, rose from the floor like ancient sentinels.

But the most striking feature was a series of smaller,

interconnected chambers branching off from the main cavern. These chambers, too, were surprisingly dry and relatively free of the moisture that permeated the rest of the system. The air within felt different, cleaner, almost sacred. Brother Etienne, his heart pounding in his chest, felt a shiver run down his spine. He knew, instinctively, that they had found what they were looking for. This was no ordinary cave system. This was a hidden sanctuary, a place perfectly suited to conceal their precious relics, a place where they could finally breathe free from the ever-present shadow of

persecution.

"Deus vult," he whispered, the words echoing softly in the vast chamber. "God wills it."

Thomas nodded, his eyes filled with a mixture of awe and relief. This discovery was more than just a safe haven; it was a miracle, an answer to their prayers. The arduous journey, the hardships endured, the constant fear – all of it seemed to melt away in the face of this unexpected blessing.

The next few days were a whirlwind of activity. Working tirelessly, the brothers began to prepare the cavern for its sacred purpose. They used their remaining tools, their

limited skills, and their unwavering faith to transform this subterranean world into a formidable fortress. The entrance to the main cavern was carefully concealed, camouflaged by ingenious booby traps designed to deter any who dared to trespass. They used strategically placed rocks, concealed tripwires, and even the natural terrain to create a labyrinthine defense system.

The smaller chambers were meticulously cleaned and prepared to house the relics. They created simple wooden shelves and chests, using materials salvaged from wrecked ships they had encountered along the way. They meticulously cataloged each item, recording its description and history in painstaking detail.

The sacred vessels, shimmering faintly in the torchlight, filled the air with a palpable sense of reverence. The chalices, once used to celebrate the Eucharist, now held a deeper significance – a symbol of faith in the face of adversity. The ancient manuscripts, their pages brittle with age, spoke of centuries of devotion, courage and sacrifice. The relics were not just objects; they were tangible links to their past, to the enduring spirit of the Knights Templar.

As they worked, the brothers exchanged quiet words of comfort, support, and gratitude. The weight of their burden began to ease, replaced by a growing sense of hope and purpose. They were no longer just fugitives, fleeing for their lives. They were guardians, protectors of a sacred legacy entrusted to their care. The task before them was enormous, but their faith and determination were stronger than ever before. They had found their new sanctuary, and within its hidden depths, they would safeguard their heritage for generations to come. The rough-hewn walls of the cave seemed to echo their silent vow – a promise whispered into the darkness, a testament to their unwavering faith and the enduring spirit of the Knights Templar. The journey was far from over, but for now, they had found peace, a fragile sanctuary in the heart of the unforgiving wilderness. Their faith was their shield, their brotherhood their sword, and the hidden cave their sanctuary, a secret held deep within the earth, a silent promise of survival.

The days turned into weeks, and the weeks into months. The brothers adapted to their new life, working tirelessly to ensure the security of their hidden sanctuary. They spent their days working, tending to their small garden, hunting and fishing for food. Their nights were filled with prayers, study, and planning. They created detailed maps of the cave system, marking secret passages and booby traps. They developed systems for communication and defense, strengthening their resolve to safeguard their holy relics.

Their days were a routine dictated by necessity. The sun's warmth served as a reminder of their past, a past that seemed a lifetime ago. Yet their spirits were far from dimmed. Their isolation fostered a unique bond among the few surviving knights, strengthening their faith and reinforcing the brotherhood that had become their only solace. They lived in a precarious existence, always aware of the potential for discovery. Yet, deep within the heart of the wilderness, they found a sense of belonging, a sense of peace they had not known since the fall of their order.

One evening, while Brother Thomas meticulously copied an ancient scroll, he heard a faint rustle in the depths of the cave. He carefully placed the scroll back into its container, his eyes alert and his hand resting on the hilt of his sword.

Slowly, cautiously, he moved towards the source of the sound, his heart pounding in his chest. He wasn't alone. A small, frightened creature scurried past, a small fox, its eyes wide with fear. The sound had been a mere trick of the ear, a reminder of the wildness that encompassed their sanctuary.

Thomas looked up to the cave ceiling, a sigh of relief escaping his lips. Their new sanctuary was safe, for now.

The journey continued, but in the silence of their hidden world, amidst the sacred relics, they would endure. Their faith, their brotherhood, and their hidden sanctuary were their shields against the storms of a turbulent world. The fight for their legacy had only just begun.

Relocating the Relics

The decision had been agonizing, a weighing of risks against the near certainty of discovery in their current, inadequate shelter. The cove, once a haven offering a semblance of concealment, now felt like a death trap, its exposed location a beacon for any who might seek the Templars' sacred burden. Brother Thomas, ever the pragmatist, had advocated for the move. His younger brother, Jean, though initially hesitant, had come to agree. The weight of responsibility, the fear of betraying the trust placed in them by the dying Grand Master, fueled their determination.

The task before them was daunting. The relics – the chalice, rumored to have been used at the Last Supper; fragments of the True Cross, each shard imbued with profound historical and spiritual significance; and the intricately carved reliquary containing a piece of the Shroud of Turin – were not easily transported. They were heavy, demanding careful handling, and their very presence demanded utmost secrecy. Their current hiding place, a damp, sea-worn cave, offered little protection against the elements, let alone the eyes of potential pursuers.

Their new sanctuary lay miles inland, a network of caves hidden deep within a dense, forbidding forest. Brother Guillaume, with his intimate knowledge of the Nova Scotian wilderness gleaned from years spent mapping the unexplored regions of the continent, had located it. It was a risky venture; the journey was treacherous, demanding stamina and resilience that tested the brothers' physical and mental limits. The path was fraught with obstacles: treacherous bogs that threatened to swallow them whole, dense thickets that clawed at their clothes and skin, and the ever-present threat of wild animals lurking in the shadows. The weight of the relics added to their burden, each step a struggle against the elements and their own fatigue.

The first leg of their journey took them through a vast,

seemingly endless swamp. The mud clung to their boots, slowing their progress to a crawl. Jean, his strength faltering under the weight of the chalice, nearly succumbed to the mire, his cry for help a choked gasp swallowed by the oppressive stillness of the swamp. Brother Thomas, ever watchful, quickly pulled him from the sucking mud, his own body straining under the exertion. They rested only briefly, the chilling damp seeping into their bones, before continuing their arduous trek.

Their only respite came at dusk, when they reached a small, rocky outcrop overlooking a rushing stream. Exhausted and soaked to the bone, they huddled together, sharing meager rations and offering prayers of thanksgiving for their continued safety. The silence was broken only by the relentless drone of insects and the mournful cry of an unseen owl, the sounds mirroring their weary hearts. The night offered little comfort; the biting chill of the Nova Scotian autumn gnawed at them, offering a harsh reminder of their isolation. But the thought of the relics, and their sacred duty to protect them, spurred them onward.

The forest proved to be an equally formidable challenge. The tangled undergrowth snagged at their clothes, tearing at their already worn garments. Twisted branches reached out like skeletal fingers, their sharp points piercing their skin. The darkness of the forest was profound, punctuated only by the occasional sliver of moonlight filtering through the dense canopy. Every rustle, every snap of a twig, sent jolts of adrenaline through their bodies, their nerves frayed by days of unrelenting pressure.

They pressed on through the darkness, their resolve
strengthened by their shared purpose. They moved in
silence, their footsteps muffled by the damp earth, each of them
acutely aware of their vulnerability. They moved as one, an inseparable
brotherhood bound by their sacred mission, their trust in each other
absolute. The shared weight of the relics felt less a burden and more a
symbol of their shared faith, a tangible link to their sacred past.

The final stretch of their journey was particularly
treacherous. They traversed a steep, rocky incline, the loose shale
threatening to send them tumbling down the hillside. They moved with
agonizing slowness, their bodies aching, their spirits tested. The weight
of the chalice, now pressing heavily on Jean's shoulders, seemed to grow
with each passing moment.

It was Brother Guillaume who noticed it first. A subtle shift in the
terrain, a change in the pattern of the trees – a sign that they were
nearing their destination. His knowledge of the land, honed over years
of solitary exploration, proved to be their salvation. As they crested the
final rise, the sight that met their eyes filled them with a mixture of
relief and awe.

Before them lay a hidden valley, shrouded in mist and
mystery, a sanctuary concealed from the prying eyes of the world.
The entrance to the cave system, partially concealed by an overhanging
rock formation, offered a sense of security and hope. This hidden
world, with its dark, echoing chambers and mysterious depths, would
be the new custodian of their sacred relics, a testament to their
unwavering faith and unwavering resolve.

The relocation of the relics was a slow, painstaking process. They carried the precious artifacts one by one, inching their

Way through the narrow passageways of the cave system. The darkness was absolute, punctuated only by the flickering light of their torches, casting dancing shadows that played tricks on their weary eyes. Each step demanded caution and precision; a single misstep could have catastrophic

consequences.

The chosen chambers were far from pristine. The air hung heavy with the scent of damp earth and something else, something ancient and indescribable. The walls were damp, the floor uneven, but the space offered sufficient protection from the elements and, more importantly, from unwanted visitors.

Securing the relics wasn't enough. They had to protect their new sanctuary. Using their skills honed in the Holy Land and their knowledge of ancient trap-making techniques, they meticulously set about creating a series of booby traps.

Hidden passages, pressure plates, and cunningly concealed tripwires would deter any intruders, protecting their sacred trust. The knowledge of their ingenuity brought a grim satisfaction. The fight for the relics was far from over, but they had given themselves a fighting chance. The forest, the swamp, the arduous journey—all served to isolate their sanctuary, to veil it in a cloak of the wild, making it almost impossible to find.

As they finished their work, a sense of profound relief

washed over them. They had successfully relocated the relics, securing them in a place of relative safety. The weight of their responsibility remained, but for now, at least, their sacred burden was safe. The exhaustion was profound, a weariness that went beyond physical fatigue and seeped into their very souls. They collapsed in the darkness, their bodies spent, but their spirits unbroken.

The dawn broke over their new sanctuary, casting long
shadows across the valley. It was a new beginning, a fresh chapter
in their desperate struggle for survival. They had lost much, but they
had also found something precious – a new sanctuary, a refuge from the
storm, a place to hold onto their faith and their legacy. The fight was far
from over, but for now, amidst the hidden depths of their new world,
they had found a place to rest, to gather their strength, and to prepare
for whatever trials lay ahead. The silent forest watched over them, a
silent guardian of their sacred trust. The wind whispered through the
trees, carrying the echoes of their prayers and their hopes for the future.
The journey had been perilous, the challenges insurmountable, but the
unshakeable brotherhood of the Templars, united in their faith, had
prevailed. The true test, however, still lay ahead.

Internal Conflict

The biting Nova Scotian wind whipped through the
makeshift encampment, carrying with it the scent of pine and
damp earth. A chilling silence had fallen over the remaining Knights
Templar, a stark contrast to the usual murmur of prayers and the
clinking of tools as they worked to further fortify their sanctuary. The
usual camaraderie, forged in the fires of persecution and hardship, felt
fractured, strained by an unspoken tension that hung heavy in the air.
Brother Thomas, usually jovial and quick with a jest, sat hunched over a
meager fire, his gaze fixed on the flames, his usually boisterous laughter
absent. Brother Etienne, ever vigilant, paced restlessly, his hand never
far from the hilt of his
sword.

The seed of distrust had been sown subtly, a whisper here, a
misplaced tool there, a discrepancy in the nightly watch roster. It had
begun with small things, easily dismissed as fatigue or the stress of
their precarious situation. But the accumulation of these minor
inconsistencies had created a chasm of doubt that threatened to shatter
the fragile unity they had managed to preserve through their arduous
journey.

The whispers, initially muted and hesitant, had grown bolder,
fueled by paranoia and the ever-present fear of betrayal.

Brother Jean-Luc, a man of unwavering faith and quiet strength,
had been the first to voice his concerns. He had noticed the subtle
shifts in behavior, the furtive glances exchanged between some of the
brothers, the carefully chosen words that hinted at something more
sinister. His observations, initially met with skepticism, were now
causing ripples of apprehension among his brothers. The

weight of their shared secret, the sacred relics hidden deep within the earth, amplified the fear, turning every shadow into a potential enemy.

"Brothers," Jean-Luc began, his voice low and grave,

addressing the small circle gathered around the fire, "we have faced the fury of the Pope, the wrath of the Inquisition, and the unforgiving wilderness. But the greatest threat may lie not in the outside world, but within our own ranks."

A murmur rippled through the group. Brother Guillaume, his face etched with weariness, spoke up. "You speak of

treachery, Jean-Luc. But among us? It seems impossible."

"Nothing is impossible, Guillaume," Etienne countered, his voice sharp. "We are hunted men, living on the edge of survival. Desperation breeds treachery." He cast a pointed glance towards Brother Alain, a man known for his quiet demeanor and seemingly unwavering loyalty. Alain flinched under his gaze, his hand instinctively going to his belt, where his dagger was concealed.

The ensuing days were filled with a heavy sense of suspicion and mistrust. Each brother became a subject of intense scrutiny. Brother Thomas, usually meticulous in his record-keeping, had seemingly made a series of careless errors.

Brother Geoffroi, always reliable, had been seen lingering near the concealed entrance to the vault more than was

necessary. Even the most trusted members of the order found themselves under a microscope.

The atmosphere was thick with tension. Conversations were clipped, punctuated by uneasy silences. The brothers, once united in their shared faith and purpose, were now divided by suspicion and fear, watching each other with wary eyes.

The bond of brotherhood, forged in the fires of hardship, was being tested to its limits.

Jean-Luc, burdened by the weight of his suspicions, initiated a clandestine investigation. He began discreetly questioning each brother, seeking inconsistencies in their accounts, searching for any evidence of treachery. He knew that he was risking further fracturing the fragile unity of their group, but he also knew that the threat of betrayal, left unchecked, could lead to their ruin.

His inquiries were met with mixed responses. Some brothers were willing to share their observations, others remained guarded, clinging to the belief that their brotherhood was beyond reproach. The lack of explicit evidence made the task even more difficult, the search for a traitor akin to searching for a needle in a haystack. Yet, Jean-Luc persevered, driven by a deep sense of duty and the conviction that if he didn't uncover the traitor, the

consequences could be devastating.

His investigation finally led him to a seemingly insignificant detail: a set of footprints near the vault's entrance, different from those of any of the brothers. These subtle clues, coupled with his observations of Alain's increasingly erratic behavior, pointed towards a shocking conclusion. Alain, despite his apparent quiet demeanor and long-standing loyalty, was the suspected traitor.

The confrontation with Alain was tense, filled with a palpable sense of dread. Alain, initially denying the accusations, eventually broke under the weight of the evidence. He confessed to his treachery, revealing a pact made with a group of mercenaries, motivated by the promise of a substantial reward for leading them to the Templar's hidden treasure.

Alain's betrayal left a deep wound on the brotherhood. The once-sacred bonds were severed, replaced by a bitter sense of betrayal and disillusionment. The Knights Templar had to confront the horrifying reality of the treachery within their ranks. The aftermath was a difficult process of healing and rebuilding trust. The surviving brothers had to navigate the pain and anger caused by Alain's betrayal and reconcile their fractured relationships. The arduous journey to rebuild trust was as challenging as their escape from Jerusalem,

demanding patience, forgiveness, and a reaffirmation of their shared commitment to protecting their legacy. The

experience left a deep scar on their community, a sobering reminder of the fragility of trust and the devastating consequences of betrayal.

In the quiet aftermath of the betrayal, the Knights Templar redoubled their efforts to secure their sanctuary. New

security measures were implemented, including enhanced watch rotations, improved booby traps, and a more rigorous system of accountability. They also strengthened their internal communication, ensuring that any future suspicions could be addressed promptly and effectively. The experience served as a harsh lesson, highlighting the importance of vigilance and the need for unwavering trust among their own. While the betrayal left a deep scar on their fellowship, it also strengthened their resolve to protect their sacred trust and their legacy, a testament to their resilience and enduring faith. The incident acted as a crucible, refining their

brotherhood and solidifying their determination to preserve the treasures entrusted to their care. The harsh realities of betrayal had tested the limits of their bonds, but the surviving Knights Templar had emerged, though wounded, stronger and more united than ever.

Unmasking the Traitor

The flickering firelight cast long, dancing shadows across the faces of the remaining Knights Templar, each man a study in grim determination. The betrayal had struck at the very heart of their brotherhood, leaving a wound that festered with suspicion and distrust. The idyllic sanctuary, once a haven of peace and shared labor, now felt like a pressure cooker, the air thick with unspoken accusations.

Brother Jean, his normally steady hand trembling slightly, meticulously examined the crude map leading to their hidden vault. It was a copy, of course, but the original had vanished, along with a significant portion of their meager supplies.

Brother Etienne, his hawk-like gaze sweeping across the assembled knights, spoke first, his voice low and gravelly,"We must find him, brothers. The traitor amongst us is a viper in our midst, slowly poisoning our fellowship." His words hung heavy in the air, punctuated only by the crackling of the fire and the rustling of the wind outside.

The investigation began subtly, a series of seemingly

innocuous observations. Brother Thomas, once their jovial leader, had become withdrawn, his eyes shadowed with an unfamiliar darkness. His usual cheerful banter was replaced by a brooding silence, his movements stiff and hesitant. The other brothers noticed it, too, the subtle changes in his demeanor, the way he seemed to avoid direct eye contact, the slight flinch when his name was mentioned.

Brother Guillaume, known for his meticulous record-keeping, painstakingly reviewed the Templar's daily logs, searching for any inconsistencies, any unusual entries that might hint at the traitor's actions. He cross-referenced the supplies inventory with the known consumption rates, meticulously detailing the discrepancies. The missing

supplies weren't insignificant—a significant portion of their winter rations were gone. Enough to weaken them

considerably and jeopardize their survival during the harsh Nova Scotian winter.

Days blurred into nights, each hour a testament to their growing unease. The Knights Templar, masters of disguise and stealth, now found themselves meticulously scrutinizing each other, their senses heightened, their trust shattered.

They were hunters, now hunted within their own ranks.

Brother Geoffroi, a master of interrogation from his days in the Holy Land, began a series of private conversations with each knight. He employed his honed skills, using subtle prompts, probing questions, carefully observing their reactions. He watched for shifts in their posture, the slight widening of their eyes, the tremor in their voice—tell-tale signs of deception. He discovered conflicting accounts of the previous night's watch schedule, minor discrepancies that, when taken together, painted a picture of possible collusion.

The tension reached a fever pitch when Brother Armand, a devout and gentle soul, confessed to having seen Brother Thomas moving towards the hidden vault late one night. He'd assumed it was a routine check, but the lateness of the hour, combined with the secrecy, had aroused his suspicions.

This piece of information, although circumstantial, was enough to shift the focus of suspicion squarely onto Brother Thomas.

However, Brother Thomas steadfastly denied any

involvement in the theft. His denials were vehement, his eyes blazing with indignation. He blamed the inconsistencies on faulty record-keeping and suggested that the supplies might have been stolen by an outside force. He insisted that his presence near the vault had been purely coincidental, a late-night prayer vigil. His unwavering denial added a further layer of complexity to the investigation.

The Knights Templar found themselves in a precarious position. Confronting Brother Thomas directly could spark a conflict, jeopardizing their already fragile unity. The repercussions of a wrongly accused brother could be

devastating, eroding the remaining trust within their ranks.

But the alternative – letting a traitor remain within their midst – was equally dangerous, potentially leading to their complete downfall.

The investigation took an unexpected turn when Brother Etienne discovered a small, almost imperceptible scratch on the lock mechanism of the vault. He meticulously compared it to the markings on the tools used by each knight. His expertise in locksmithing, acquired over years of securing Templar treasures, allowed him to isolate the tool that had made the scratch. The mark belonged to a tool in Brother Thomas's possession.

This seemingly small piece of evidence, however, proved to be irrefutable. Faced with the undeniable proof, Brother Thomas finally broke down, his meticulously constructed facade crumbling. He confessed, his voice choked with remorse, to stealing the map and the supplies. His confession was not driven by greed or malice but rather by a deep-seated fear. He had been tormented by nightmares, haunted by the horrors he'd witnessed during the Crusades, the constant fear of persecution and death. He had believed that he could protect the remaining brothers by taking the

precious map and supplies to a remote location, and only he could return later if they were discovered. His misguided attempt at safeguarding them had been interpreted as treachery. While his intentions were noble, his actions were

undoubtedly wrong. His confession, though painful, brought a semblance of closure, a resolution to the tense atmosphere that had been suffocating their brotherhood. His act of self-preservation had almost broken the very bond he had tried so desperately to protect. In the aftermath of the confession, the brotherhood began a slow process of healing. They held a solemn ceremony, expressing their forgiveness, their commitment to rebuilding the shattered trust. They were well aware that the dangers they still faced in the unforgiving Nova Scotian wilderness, were multiplied by the threat of any future betrayals. Their unity had been tested, almost broken, but in the end, their bond endured. The experience served as a solemn reminder of the importance of vigilance, and the paramount need for unwavering faith and loyalty amidst adversity. They had survived the loss, and the betrayal, and from the ashes of the incident, emerged stronger and more united. The harsh winds of betrayal had failed to shatter their resolve; instead, they had forged their brotherhood anew, ready to face the uncertainties that lay ahead. The journey to secure their legacy was far from over, but their unity, once almost lost, was once again their

strength, a beacon guiding them through the dark unknown.

The sacred treasures remained safe, guarded not only by booby traps and fortifications, but by the enduring bond of brotherhood, tested and refined in the crucible of betrayal.

The Price of Treason

The morning light, weak and watery, struggled to pierce the gloom of the makeshift chapel carved into the cliff face. Brother Thomas, his face etched with a weariness that belied his youthful appearance, knelt before the makeshift altar, a rough-hewn slab of stone. He muttered a silent prayer, his gaze fixed on a small, tarnished silver crucifix. The betrayal still hung heavy in the air, a suffocating shroud woven from suspicion and unspoken accusations. The theft of the map, the missing supplies – these were tangible losses, but the erosion of trust, the shattering of their sacred bond, was a wound that ran far deeper.

He rose, his joints creaking in protest, and walked towards the crudely constructed dwelling where Brother Etienne, the suspected traitor, was being held. Etienne, usually jovial and boisterous, sat hunched in a corner, his face pale and drawn, his eyes filled with a mixture of defiance and despair. He hadn't spoken since his capture, a stubborn silence that only amplified the gravity of his crime.

Brother Thomas paused at the entrance, his hand resting on the rough-hewn wooden door. He had expected anger, a burning desire for vengeance. Instead, a profound sadness washed over him. Etienne, despite his actions, was still one of them, bound by the same vows, the same unwavering faith in God and the Templar order. The price of treason, however, was steep, and it couldn't be paid with mere sorrow.

He pushed open the door, the sound echoing in the confined space. Etienne looked up, his gaze meeting Thomas's with a flicker of something akin to fear.

"Etienne," Thomas began, his voice low and measured, "We have found evidence. The map... the missing supplies... it all points to you. You betrayed us."

Etienne flinched, but remained silent, his gaze fixed on the ground. Thomas continued, his voice softening slightly. "Why, Etienne? Why would you do this to us? To your brothers?"

The silence stretched, thick and suffocating. Then, a ragged sigh escaped Etienne's lips. He began to speak, his voice a barely audible whisper, his words tumbling out in a torrent of confession and remorse. He spoke of desperation, of the gnawing fear that they would not survive the harsh winter, of the agonizing pangs of hunger that had driven him to a point of near madness. He hadn't intended to betray them, he claimed; he'd only sought to secure their survival. He had planned to return with supplies from a nearby settlement, a settlement he knew well from past travels. He'd hoped to obtain supplies he believed would be enough for them all, a chance to save their lives, but only now he understood his mistake.

He spoke of his family, his aging mother, his young sister, living far from his reach, and the fear that had propelled him to this act of desperation. He had envisioned a future where he would provide for them, where he could return with food and help his family survive the harsh winter in his homeland.

He'd believed, even as he'd committed the act, that his intentions could somehow justify his means.

His words were a tangled web of justifications and remorse, but behind them, Thomas saw a flicker of genuine sorrow, a desperate plea for understanding. The betrayal was undeniable, but its origins lay in a complex web of fear, desperation, and misplaced loyalty. Etienne hadn't acted out of malice, but out of a profound love for his family, a love that had twisted his sense of right and wrong, blurring the lines between survival and betrayal.

Thomas listened patiently, his heart heavy with a mixture of sympathy and condemnation. He understood the desperation, the weight of responsibility that had crushed Etienne's spirit, but he also understood the gravity of his actions. The betrayal had threatened not only their physical survival but the very soul of their brotherhood. The trust, so painstakingly rebuilt after Brother Jean's confession, had been shattered again, leaving them more vulnerable than before. The price of treason was high, and it was far beyond Etienne's simple explanation.

The discussion continued into the late afternoon, the

flickering firelight casting long shadows on the walls of the makeshift dwelling. Thomas spoke of the consequences, of the need for justice, and of the importance of maintaining order and discipline within their small community. Etienne, broken and humbled, listened silently, accepting his fate with a quiet dignity. There were no outbursts of anger, no dramatic scenes of vengeance. Instead, a somber acceptance hung in the air, a recognition of the harsh realities of their situation and the price of survival in this unforgiving land.

The decision reached that night, under the pale light of the moon, was not one of anger or revenge, but of solemn justice. Etienne, stripped of his Templar robes, was sentenced to exile. He was given provisions for his journey, a small sum of money, and a heartfelt blessing from Brother Thomas, a blessing filled with sadness and a touch of forgiveness. The weight of his actions and their consequences were heavy, a burden he would bear for the rest of his days.

His exile was not a punishment inflicted in anger, but a

necessity, a way to safeguard the remaining brotherhood from any further doubt or suspicion. The brothers were fully aware that his crime, however understandable, was a potentially fatal threat to their survival. His act of

desperation could have led to their downfall, leaving them open to attack or starvation. While forgiveness was offered, there was a harsh understanding that, at some point, justice must be served and trust, once broken, must be repaired cautiously. The loss of Etienne, though painful, was seen as a necessary sacrifice to preserve the fragile unity that was their only defense against the harsh realities of their existence in Nova Scotia. The bond of brotherhood was strengthened through this pain, and the memory of Etienne's betrayal served as a reminder of the unwavering loyalty required to survive and to safeguard their sacred legacy.

The remaining knights held a vigil that night, not only to acknowledge Etienne's exile, but also to reaffirm their

commitment to each other. They lit candles and prayed, seeking guidance and strength from God in their hour of need. The pain of the betrayal still lingered, but they knew that they had to move forward, that their survival depended on their unity and their unwavering faith. The journey ahead was perilous, filled with challenges and dangers, but they faced it together, their brotherhood strengthened by the ordeal they had faced. The price of treason had been paid, but the scars it left would remain, a constant reminder of the fragility of trust and the vital importance of unwavering loyalty. The memory of Etienne's act would serve as both a warning and a lesson, a testament to the devastating consequences of desperation and a reminder that the pursuit of survival, while essential, must always be tempered with the principles of faith and brotherly love. Their sacred

mission, and the protection of the relics, relied upon the

strength of their brotherhood, now more tested, and in a way, more unified than ever. The weight of their past, the urgency of their present, and the uncertainty of their future continued to shape their destiny, but their renewed resolve burned brightly, a beacon in the darkness of their challenging

circumstances.

Rebuilding Trust

The days that followed Etienne's expulsion were marked by a cautious silence, a fragile peace built on the ashes of betrayal. The rhythmic clang of the blacksmith's hammer, usually a comforting sound, now felt discordant, a jarring reminder of the fractured brotherhood. Brother Thomas, his youthful face etched with worry lines far beyond his years, found himself mediating more disputes than forging weapons. Minor disagreements over rations, the division of labor, even the seemingly insignificant task of gathering firewood, became flashpoints, fueled by the lingering

suspicion and unspoken resentments.

Sir Geoffroi, the oldest and most experienced of the knights, took it upon himself to address the simmering tension. He called a meeting under the ancient, gnarled branches of a giant oak, its leaves rustling like whispers in the wind. The knights gathered, their faces grim, their eyes guarded. The air hung heavy with the unspoken questions, the accusations that dared not be voiced.

"Brothers," Geoffroi began, his voice raspy but firm, "we stand at a precipice. Etienne's actions have shaken us to our core, but they cannot break us. We are Knights Templar, bound by a sacred oath, a brotherhood forged in the fires of faith and tested by the crucible of war. We have faced death itself in the Holy Land, and we will face this trial as well.

But we cannot do it alone. We must rebuild the trust that Etienne shattered."

His words hung in the air, heavy with the weight of expectation. Several knights shifted uncomfortably, their gazes fixed on the ground. The silence that followed was punctuated only by the chirping of crickets and the distant cry of a hawk.

Brother Jean, known for his fiery temper and unwavering loyalty, spoke first, his voice tight with emotion. "How can we trust again, Sir Geoffroi? How can we forget the fear, the uncertainty, of not knowing who amongst us might turn on us? Etienne was one of us."

Geoffroi nodded, understanding the pain in Jean's words. "We cannot forget, Brother Jean, but we can learn. We must examine our own hearts and ask ourselves why Etienne felt compelled to betray us. Was it desperation? Fear? Did we, in our own way, contribute to his despair?"

A murmur rippled through the assembled knights. The

question hung heavy, forcing them to confront their own failings, their own shortcomings. They had been so focused on their mission, on the protection of the relics, that they had neglected to nurture the bonds of brotherhood, allowing cracks to form in their unity. Etienne's betrayal was not just an act of individual treachery, but a symptom of a deeper malaise.

The discussion that followed was long and arduous, a painful process of self-reflection and reconciliation. Each knight, in turn, spoke of their fears, their doubts, and their anxieties. They shared their vulnerabilities, exposing the cracks in their armor, the hidden wounds that had festered in silence. The stolen map became a symbol of their collective failure, a reminder of their oversight, of their inability to anticipate the depth of Etienne's desperation. The missing supplies served as another example of the growing disunity, each knight blaming himself and others for the lax security that allowed Etienne to act without detection.

Slowly, painstakingly, they began to rebuild the bridges that Etienne's actions had destroyed. They shared stories of their past, remembering the camaraderie and shared experiences that had forged their brotherhood. They prayed together, seeking solace and strength in their shared faith. Brother Thomas, with his gentle spirit and keen observational skills, emerged as a quiet leader, mediating disputes, fostering understanding, and reminding them of the sacred vows that bound them together.

The task of rebuilding trust was not easy. The scars of

Etienne's betrayal ran deep. Mistrust lingered, shadows of doubt danced in the corners of their eyes. But as days turned into weeks, and weeks into months, the knights slowly began to mend their fractured bonds. They learned to communicate more openly, to share their burdens, and to support each other in times of need. They discovered a new depth of understanding and compassion, forging a brotherhood

stronger and more resilient than before.

One evening, as the sun dipped below the horizon, painting the sky in hues of orange and purple, Sir Geoffroi gathered the knights once more. He held a small, worn leather-bound book, the Templar Rule, its pages yellowed with age.

"Brothers," he said, his voice filled with emotion, "this book contains the principles by which we live, the vows we have sworn. It speaks of faith, courage, and loyalty, but also of humility, compassion, and forgiveness. We have faltered, but we have also learned. Let this book be a reminder of our sacred duty, a testament to the strength of our brotherhood, and a guide for the journey that lies ahead."

He opened the book, and as he read the ancient words, a profound sense of unity settled over the assembled knights. The weight of their past, the pain of their betrayal, did not disappear completely. But they had learned from it. They had faced their vulnerabilities, and in doing so, they had found a new strength, a renewed sense of purpose. They were no longer just survivors; they were a brotherhood reborn, tempered in the crucible of adversity, united in their faith, and prepared to face whatever challenges lay ahead. The journey to Nova Scotia remained dangerous, fraught with peril. But now, they faced it as one, their brotherhood stronger, their resolve unshaken, their spirits renewed. The ghosts of the past would always linger, a solemn reminder of the fragility of trust, but the flame of their fellowship burned brightly, illuminating the path towards their shared destiny. The relics remained their sacred charge, but the preservation of their brotherhood had become equally, if not more,

important. Their mission was not simply to protect the relics; it was to protect each other, to honor their vows, and to carry on the legacy of the Knights Templar. The road ahead remained long and arduous, filled with challenges and uncertainties. Yet, as they looked at each other, a quiet understanding passed between them; they would face it together, united not just by their shared purpose, but by the strengthened bonds of brotherhood they had painstakingly rebuilt. They had faced death, betrayal, and the shattering of their trust, but they had emerged stronger, their faith unwavering, their resolve hardened, their brotherhood renewed – prepared to face whatever lay ahead. The journey towards Nova Scotia was far from over, but they were finally ready, finally united, and ready to continue their mission.

Strengthening Security

The salt spray stung their faces as the battered ship,

The Wanderer

, sliced through the turbulent Atlantic. The ordeal in Europe felt a lifetime ago, a horrific dream from which they had only recently awakened. Yet, the memory of

Etienne's treachery, the chilling ease with which he had betrayed their sacred trust, remained a sharp, persistent pain.

Brother Thomas, ever practical, had begun to implement a series of security measures designed to prevent such a

betrayal from ever occurring again. The first change was subtle yet significant: a complete restructuring of their

internal communication. Previously, information had flowed relatively freely, a testament to their once unwavering trust.

Now, a rigid system of encrypted messages and carefully controlled access to sensitive information was in place. Only Brother Thomas, as the newly appointed Master of the Order, possessed the full picture. The others received only the information pertinent to their specific tasks, meticulously compartmentalized to limit the damage of any future betrayal.

This new system extended beyond simple messaging. The division of labor, once fairly fluid, was now strictly defined.

Each brother had a specific role, with clearly delineated responsibilities and limited cross-over. This prevented any single individual from gaining a complete understanding of their mission or having access to all of the sacred relics. The relics themselves, once relatively accessible, were now encased in multiple layers of protection. Each item was individually secured within a water-tight, tamper-proof container, further protected by a complex system of locks and keys, each held by a different brother. The keys were themselves concealed within an even more intricate series of compartments within the ship's hull. Only in the event of the utmost emergency – and with the unanimous agreement of the remaining brothers – could the relics be retrieved.

Brother Giles, the group's historian and keeper of ancient texts, meticulously documented every decision, every action taken, and every piece of information exchanged. His records, hidden within a series of water-resistant scrolls concealed in a hollowed-out section of the ship's mast, were meant to provide a complete record of their journey should any catastrophe befall the brothers. They also served as a vital piece of the new security structure, allowing for an audit trail in case of suspected treachery. Furthermore, Brother Giles was tasked with developing a more sophisticated system of coded messages, a complex cipher that would defy interception and decryption, ensuring that their communications remained confidential.

Beyond the organizational changes, Brother Thomas implemented physical security enhancements. They were no longer merely refugees, but hardened warriors guarding a sacred trust. While the ocean provided some measure of protection, they knew they had to stay vigilant. Night watches were doubled, and the brothers were trained in advanced defensive tactics. Each brother was assigned a specific watch position, ensuring complete coverage. They rotated positions frequently, preventing complacency and maintaining a state of heightened alertness. Their weaponry was also upgraded. In addition to their swords and other traditional arms, they acquired more powerful weaponry: crossbows with advanced quarrel mechanisms for long-range defense, and hidden daggers for close-quarters combat. The ship itself was reinforced, vulnerable areas patched, and extra supplies of food, water, and ammunition were secured, to endure a lengthy siege if need be.

The journey was long and arduous, each day a test of their resilience. Storms lashed against

The Wanderer

, threatening to shatter the ship and send them all to watery graves. But the storms tested more than the ship's strength. They tested the renewed unity amongst the brothers. The shared danger and the constant threat forged a stronger bond. They discovered a different resilience than that forged in the fires of betrayal. This resilience found strength in mutual support and shared understanding. The constant vigilance, the

rigorous security protocols, and the knowledge of the

devastating consequences of failure solidified their shared purpose. Each brother understood the stakes involved in their mission, that failure would not only cost them their lives, but also the legacy of the Knights Templar, a legacy that spanned centuries.

The constant vigilance also sharpened their senses. They had learned to read the subtle signs of danger, to interpret the nuances of the ocean's moods, and to anticipate threats before they materialized. The sea was their ally, but also a potential adversary. Every passing ship, every distant sail, was initially viewed with suspicion. Yet, the constant scanning of the horizon, the repetitive checks of their defenses, did not quell a profound feeling of solitude. They were adrift in a vast ocean, cut off from the rest of the world, hunted by those who sought to destroy them. The silence of the sea was often more terrifying than the roar of the storm, the vast emptiness a constant reminder of their isolation and the weight of their responsibility.

Brother Thomas, however, remained resolute. His leadership was not tyrannical, but rather firm and compassionate. He understood the psychological toll of their ordeal, the burden of fear and suspicion. He instituted regular periods of reflection and prayer, providing a much-needed respite from the constant pressure of their situation. These moments allowed the brothers to reconnect with their faith, to reinforce their shared belief, and to reaffirm their commitment to their mission. They shared stories of their past, of the brotherhood they had once known, of the ideals that had driven them, and of the unwavering faith that had sustained them through unimaginable hardship. These moments of shared vulnerability helped to rebuild the trust that had been so brutally shattered, forging a stronger, more resilient bond than they had ever imagined possible.

Despite the hardships, they pressed on, their spirits tempered by their shared experiences. The days bled into weeks, the weeks into months. They learned to work together seamlessly, anticipating each other's needs, providing support when needed. The constant threat of discovery became a shared reality, and it was not a threat that weakened them, but one that strengthened their bonds of brotherhood. They were no longer just knights; they were family, bound together not by blood, but by faith, by a common purpose, and by the harrowing ordeal they had endured together. They were a brotherhood reborn, forged in the crucible of betrayal and tempered by the unrelenting challenges of their perilous journey. Their new security measures were more than just physical safeguards; they were a testament to the strength of their renewed fellowship, a symbol of their unwavering commitment to protect their sacred relics and their legacy. Their journey was not only a race against time and those who sought to destroy them, but a race to solidify and strengthen their brotherhood, a task that proved to be as challenging, and as important, as their central mission. The ocean stretched ahead, vast and unforgiving, yet they moved forward, united, prepared for whatever the future held. The ghost of Etienne's betrayal still lingered, a constant reminder of the fragility of trust, but it was a reminder that fueled their vigilance and strengthened their resolve. They were survivors, not just of the treacherous seas, but of the even more treacherous currents of human betrayal. And they were ready.

The Inevitable Confrontation

The biting Nova Scotian wind whipped around Brother Thomas, stinging his cheeks and carrying the scent of pine and damp earth. He clutched his worn leather-bound prayer book, its pages brittle with age, a testament to the years of hardship he and his brethren had endured since fleeing Jerusalem. The air crackled with a tension thicker than the encroaching twilight. For months, they had lived in the shadow of the Inquisition, their every step a gamble, their every breath a prayer. Now, the gamble was over. The inevitable had arrived.

A distant crackle of branches, then the unmistakable thud of boots on frozen ground broke the chilling silence. Brother Thomas exchanged a grim look with Brother Etienne, their faces etched with the weariness of a long and brutal flight.

Their small band, once a proud company of knights, was now a mere handful of survivors, their numbers thinned by disease, starvation, and the relentless pursuit of their

enemies. Yet, in their eyes burned a defiant fire, a stubborn refusal to surrender their sacred trust – the relics entrusted to their care, the legacy of the Templar Order.

The sound of approaching men grew louder, closer. From their hidden vantage point, nestled amongst the ancient redwoods, they could make out the glint of steel in the fading light. The Inquisitors. Their pursuers had finally caught up. This was it. The final stand.

Brother Thomas felt a surge of adrenaline, a familiar mix of fear and resolve. He had faced death before, on the

battlefields of the Holy Land, but this felt different. This wasn't a glorious crusade, a righteous war against infidels.

This was a desperate fight for survival, a last-ditch effort to protect a legacy that stretched back centuries. The weight of history rested on his shoulders, heavy as the armor he no longer wore.

As the Inquisitors emerged from the trees, their numbers far exceeding their own, a chilling wave of despair washed over him. Yet, alongside the fear, a resolute determination hardened his gaze. He would not let the legacy of the Templars be extinguished. He would fight to his last breath, a testament to the unwavering faith and courage of his Order. He looked at his brothers, their faces grim but resolute, their eyes reflecting the same unyielding spirit.

The first volley of arrows rained down from the trees, a hail of steel that found its mark amongst the Inquisitors. The clash of steel echoed through the silent forest as the

Templars, outnumbered but undeterred, met their pursuers with a fury born of desperation. Swords clashed, shields splintered, and the air filled with the cries of men in mortal combat. Brother Etienne, a seasoned warrior, fought with the grace and precision of a seasoned master, his blade a blur of motion. Brother Jean, though younger, fought with the ferocity of a cornered animal, his every strike fueled by a burning desire to protect his brethren.

Brother Thomas himself engaged in the fray, his every move precise and deadly. Years of training had honed his skills, turning him into a lethal warrior. Yet, even his skill could not overcome the sheer weight of numbers. The Inquisitors pressed forward, their relentless advance slowly but surely pushing the Templars back. The battle was a brutal dance of death, a grim waltz of steel and blood. One by one, the Templars fell, their bodies littering the frozen ground, their blood staining the snow a grim crimson.

Brother Jean was the first to fall, pierced through the heart by an Inquisitor's lance. His eyes, filled with a mixture of shock and regret, glazed over as life ebbed away. Brother Etienne, fighting valiantly, suffered a brutal blow to the head, his once-sharp movements now clumsy and weak. He fought on, his resolve undiminished, but his body betrayed him. He fell, his final breath escaping in a ragged gasp.

Brother Thomas watched his brethren fall, the reality of their dwindling numbers chilling him to the bone. His heart ached with grief and despair, yet he fought on. He knew he couldn't win this battle. He knew that their numbers were too few, their strength too depleted to hold off the relentless wave of the Inquisition's forces. But he would not surrender. He would fight until his dying breath.

He engaged with one of the Inquisitors, a hulking brute whose face was contorted with rage. They fought with a savagery born of desperation, their blades clashing in a deadly ballet of death. Thomas, though weary and wounded, fought with a renewed ferocity. He parried a blow, a deep cut slicing across his arm, and retaliated with a strike to the brute's leg, sending him to his knees. He pressed his advantage, his blade flashing, finally ending the Inquisitor's life with a final, fatal thrust.

He stood panting, his body racked with pain, his sword dripping blood. Around him, the battle raged on. But there were only a few Templars left, and he was the only one still standing. He knew the end was near.

As he glanced around at his fallen brethren, he saw the determination and unwavering resolve in their lifeless eyes. They had fought with courage and honor, their commitment to their order unwavering. Their sacrifice would not be in vain. Their legacy would live on.

Suddenly, the battle stopped. The sound of clashing steel faded, replaced by an eerie silence. He looked up and saw the remaining Inquisitors retreating into the forest, disappearing into the shadows. They had won. But it was a pyrrhic victory. The cost had been too high. Their numbers were decimated.

He stood there, alone amongst the fallen, the silence of the forest broken only by the mournful whisper of the wind. He knelt beside Brother Etienne, closing his eyes in prayer. He looked at the relics, still hidden, safe, his mission completed, even in defeat.

The fight was over, but the struggle wasn't. The survival of the Templar order, the protection of the sacred relics, now rested on the shoulders of the few who still lived, a weight heavier than any armor. The true fight had just begun. The fight to keep their faith, their secrets, and their very existence alive in the harsh wilderness of Nova Scotia. The struggle would continue, and their legacy would be one of survival, sacrifice, and unwavering faith. The echoes of their final stand would reverberate through time, a testament to their courage and their relentless fight to preserve their sacred heritage. The legacy of the Knights Templar would not be easily extinguished.

A Desperate Battle

The first arrow found its mark in Brother Geoffrey's

shoulder, a searing pain that ripped through the quietude of the forest. The cry that escaped his lips was swallowed by the roar of the approaching Inquisitors, their shouts a chilling counterpoint to the crackle of the flames licking at the base of the ancient oak where the Templars had made their last stand. The clearing, once a sanctuary of peace, was now a battlefield, a canvas splashed with crimson against the muted greens and browns of the Nova Scotian wilderness.

Brother Thomas, his face grim and resolute, raised his

sword, its polished steel reflecting the flickering firelight. He had witnessed the slaughter of countless brothers, seen their unwavering faith tested and broken in the fires of persecution. Yet, here, in this desolate corner of the new world, he found himself facing the same grim reaper, his resolve hardened by years of relentless pursuit. He moved with the precision born of years of training, his every movement a testament to the Templar code, a dance of death orchestrated by faith and fueled by despair.

The Inquisitors, a motley crew of mercenaries and zealots, surged forward, their armor gleaming under the moonlight, their faces contorted in a mixture of fanaticism and bloodlust. They were a formidable force, far outnumbering the remaining Templars, their numbers a stark reminder of the dwindling hope of their sacred mission. Yet, the Templars fought with the ferocity of cornered wolves, their small band a wall of steel and faith against the relentless tide.

Brother Alain, despite a deep gash across his arm, continued to fight, his movements fluid and deadly. He had been the master swordsman of their order, and even now, weakened, he danced with the death-dealing dance of the blade, his sword singing a song of defiance that echoed through the trees. His every strike was precise and powerful, a testament to his mastery and the unwavering loyalty that bound him to his brethren.

Each fallen Templar was a blow to their already waning strength, each agonizing cry a reminder of the price of their unwavering faith. Yet, they refused to yield. The sacred relics, concealed deep within the earth, were their sole reason to live. They had sworn an oath to protect these treasures, a sacred responsibility that transcended their own mortality. They were guardians of faith, protectors of history, and they would not falter, no matter the cost.

The fight raged on, a brutal ballet of steel and blood under the watchful eyes of the indifferent moon. Brother Etienne, despite being outnumbered, fought with the courage of a lion, his shield raised high, deflecting blows that would have shattered lesser men. His body was a testament to the harshness of their journey, the scars a map of their suffering, yet his spirit remained unbroken. The weight of the fight was almost unbearable, yet he continued to defend his brothers and their sacred trust.

Brother Thomas, ever vigilant, observed the battlefield, his eyes scanning for opportunities, for weaknesses in the Inquisitors' ranks. He saw a momentary lapse in their formation, a flicker of hesitation that gave him a chance to strike. With a shout, he charged, cutting through their lines like a storm, his sword a blur of motion, leaving a trail of fallen men in his wake.

His brothers, sensing his momentum, joined the fray, a renewed wave of defiance washing over the battlefield. For a brief, glorious moment, the Templar's outnumbered force fought with such ferocity that they pushed back the tide of the Inquisition. Yet, the relentless pressure of the larger force soon told. One by one, brothers fell, their fallen bodies marking the ground like tombstones in a desperate graveyard.

The fighting continued through the night. As dawn approached, the dwindling number of surviving Knights Templars were exhausted but unyielding. Their hope seemed to have disappeared, leaving only a flicker of their faith remaining. The relentless attack had taken its toll. Blood soaked the ground, and the air hung thick with the stench of death. Brother Thomas, his body battered and bruised, knew the battle was lost. Their numbers were too few, their strength too depleted.

However, even in defeat, the Templar spirit would not be broken. Brother Thomas, despite the agony tearing through his body, rallied his surviving brothers, their battered forms a testament to the tenacity of their faith. They stood together, back to back, their swords raised in a final defiant stand.

They had fought bravely, protecting their sacred relics, upholding their oaths. Their legacy was etched in blood and courage, and though their bodies might fall, their spirit would endure.

The Inquisitors, exhausted but triumphant, surrounded them, their weapons poised to deliver the final blow. But as they moved in, a different kind of fear filled their faces. The Templars, despite their dire situation, maintained a fierce determination; a look of serene confidence settled upon their faces. The Inquisitors paused, sensing something beyond the physical exhaustion of the knights.

In that moment, Brother Thomas knew that the fight for their survival extended beyond the battle itself. The true fight lay ahead, in the preservation of their faith, their legacy, and their memories. They had lost the battle, but the war, the war for their existence, was far from over. Their secret, their faith, their legacy would not be easily extinguished. Their sacrifice would become a legend whispered through time, a testament to their enduring courage and unwavering loyalty.

The final moments were swift and brutal. One by one, the Knights Templar fell, their bodies adding to the already macabre tapestry of the battlefield. The last surviving Templar, Brother Thomas, stood amidst the carnage, his breath coming in ragged gasps, his body screaming in pain.

He held his sword high, a defiant gesture against the

approaching Inquisitors. His eyes, though weary, held a spark of defiance, a testament to the indomitable spirit of the Knights Templar.

As the Inquisitors closed in, Brother Thomas closed his eyes, his final breath a silent prayer for the protection of his sacred trust. His fall marked not an end, but a transition – the beginning of a new, clandestine struggle to preserve their heritage and the legacy of the Knights Templar, a legacy born from faith, forged in fire, and destined to endure, echoing through the ages. The echoes of their desperate battle, their sacrifice, their unwavering faith – all this would be interwoven into the fabric of history, a testament to their courage and the enduring spirit of the Knights Templar. The fight for their faith, for their secrets, for their very existence had just begun, in a new land, under a new sky, a legacy waiting to be discovered.

Heavy Losses

The stench of woodsmoke and blood hung heavy in the air, a grim perfume clinging to the ravaged clearing. The battle, fierce and brutal, had left its mark – a tapestry woven with the threads of death and despair. Where moments before the ancient oak had stood sentinel over a small band of brothers, now lay a scattering of broken bodies, their Templar crosses dulled by the crimson stain of their spilled blood. The relentless assault of the Inquisitors had broken through their defenses, a tide of steel and fury that had swept away their carefully constructed barricades.

Brother Etienne, his face streaked with grime and blood, stumbled back, his sword arm hanging limp. An arrow, feathered and wicked, had found its mark, piercing the thick leather of his jerkin and lodging deep within his flesh. He leaned heavily against the rough bark of a fallen tree, the pain a dull throb that overshadowed the roar of battle now fading into a mournful sigh. Around him, the scene was a macabre tableau. Brother Jean, his eyes glazed over, lay sprawled amidst a tangle of limbs and broken weapons, a testament to the ferocity of the attack. His once-proud bearing was gone, replaced by the stillness of death.

The numbers of the Inquisitors were overwhelming. Their relentless advance, a relentless wave crashing against the dwindling ranks of the Templars, had shattered their initial resistance. Brother Guillaume, a veteran of countless battles, fought with a desperate courage that belied his weakening body. His sword, honed to a razor's edge, flashed in the dim light, deflecting blows and seeking gaps in the enemy's ranks. But even his skill, honed over years of conflict, could not hold back the tide.

Brother Armand, ever the pragmatist, had attempted a flanking maneuver, hoping to disrupt the Inquisitors' momentum. He had moved with the swiftness and grace of a woodland creature, disappearing into the shadows only to emerge, striking with deadly precision before vanishing once more. However, the Inquisitors, seasoned warriors themselves, were not easily fooled. They encircled him, trapping him in a deadly net of swords and spears. His valiant efforts bought precious time, but ultimately, he fell under the weight of superior numbers.

The few remaining Templars huddled together, their faces etched with a grim determination. Their initial hope, a flicker of defiance in the face of overwhelming odds, was now dimming, replaced by a chilling acceptance of their fate.

They were outnumbered, outmaneuvered, and surrounded.

Escape seemed impossible. Yet, they stood their ground, their unwavering faith in God a shield against the despair that threatened to engulf them.

Brother Anselm, the youngest of their number, clutched a small, worn leather-bound book to his chest – a sacred text containing ancient prayers and rituals. His eyes, wide with a mixture of fear and determination, darted around the clearing, searching for any sign of hope, any sliver of a chance for survival. He knew that their chances were slim, but he clung to the belief that a miracle might yet occur.

Despite their losses, a quiet dignity permeated their ranks.

There were no whimpers, no pleas for mercy. They faced their fate with a stoicism born of faith and brotherhood, their resolve unyielding. Their faces, grim and resolute, were set in silent prayer, their final moments echoing with the profound belief in their sacred cause.

The leader of the Inquisitors, a cruel and ruthless man named Brother Sebastian, approached slowly, his eyes cold and calculating. He had witnessed the bravery of the Templars, their unwavering defiance, and it both fascinated and angered him. He was acutely aware that the capture of these men, the end of their desperate stand, was a victory of colossal significance – their secrets, their treasures, their history all within his grasp.

Brother Sebastian surveyed the carnage, a twisted smirk playing on his lips. He raised his hand, and the remaining Inquisitors moved closer, their swords and spears glinting menacingly in the fading light. The last stand of the Knights Templar in this remote corner of the Nova Scotian wilderness was about to conclude. The weight of history, the legacy of their order, was about to be extinguished, or so he believed.

But as the Inquisitors closed in, a sudden, desperate cry pierced the silence. It was not a cry of surrender, but a defiant roar, a last surge of defiance in the face of death. Brother Guillaume, miraculously still alive despite grievous wounds, used the last of his strength to trigger a hidden mechanism. A deafening roar followed; the earth trembled, and a large section of the ancient oak, painstakingly rigged with explosive charges, crashed down, burying several Inquisitors under a mountain of splintered wood and earth.

The unexpected chaos, the sudden disruption of the Inquisitors' advance, bought the remaining Templars a few precious moments. Taking advantage of the confusion, Brother Anselm, with the agility of a mountain cat, snatched a pouch filled with a potent, sleep-inducing powder from his tunic and flung it with lethal precision into the midst of the enemy ranks. The powder exploded, creating a cloud of fine dust that swiftly engulfed the Inquisitors, its potent effect taking hold within seconds.

As the last of the Inquisitors succumbed to the cloud, and the echoes of the collapsing oak still hung in the air, Brother Etienne, gathering his last strength, whispered, "God wills it. Our secrets remain safe." His eyes closed. He had fought to his last breath, to the very edge of his endurance, and he fell, joining his fallen brothers. The battle was over, but the legacy of the Knights Templar, their unwavering faith, their sacred secrets, would live on, preserved against the cruel hands of history. The ground was littered with the fallen, Templar and Inquisitor alike, a silent testament to a battle fought with unmatched courage, and a legacy preserved amidst death and destruction. The silence of the wilderness was broken only by the gentle rustling of leaves, and the faint sigh of the wind whispering through the branches of the ravaged forest. The fight was far from over. The surviving Templars, diminished in number but undeterred in spirit, knew their mission had only just begun. Their journey,

perilous and uncertain, was far from its end. The quest to safeguard their sacred trust would continue, a testament to their enduring faith, a legacy to echo through the ages.

Protecting the Legacy

The wind, a mournful soprano, sang through the skeletal remains of the oak, whistling a dirge for the fallen. Brother Thomas, his face streaked with grime and blood, knelt beside the lifeless form of Brother Etienne, his hand resting gently on the still chest. The weight of the fallen pressed heavily upon him – a physical and emotional burden that threatened to crush him. He had witnessed too much death, too much brutality, in too short a span. Yet, the unwavering gaze of the dying Etienne, the quiet dignity in his final moments, fueled a spark of defiance within him. Etienne's last words, "God wills it. Our secrets remain safe," echoed in his mind, a battle cry against despair.

He looked around at the ravaged clearing. The earth was stained crimson, the air thick with the metallic tang of blood. The bodies of their brothers, and those of their pursuers, lay scattered amongst the broken branches and shattered remnants of their makeshift fortifications. The Inquisitors, relentless and merciless, had exacted a terrible price. But they had failed in their ultimate goal. The sacred relics, the heart of their mission, remained hidden, safeguarded by the earth and the cunning traps they had so meticulously devised.

Brother Thomas rose, his joints stiff and aching. He surveyed the remaining brothers, their faces etched with grief, exhaustion, and a grim determination. They were few, but they were not broken. The fire of their faith, though dimmed by loss, still flickered within them. Their commitment to their sacred trust, to the legacy of the Knights Templar, burned stronger than ever. This was not the end, but a turning point. The true test of their faith, their courage, their resolve, lay ahead.

Their immediate priority was the burial of their fallen

brethren. It was a solemn task, performed under the somber gaze of the twilight sky. They dug shallow graves, their movements slow and deliberate, each shovelful of earth a heavy weight on their already burdened souls. They offered prayers, whispered blessings, and murmured words of comfort, attempting to find solace in the face of such profound loss. They placed simple wooden crosses, carved hastily from salvaged branches, to mark the final resting places of their comrades, their humble tributes to the fallen guardians of their faith.

As darkness descended, they gathered around a meager fire, the flames casting flickering shadows on their weary faces.

Food was scarce, their supplies dwindling after the brutal battle. But they ate what they had, sharing their meager portions with a quiet camaraderie that transcended their exhaustion. The silence that followed was heavy with

unspoken grief, yet punctuated by the crackling of the fire, a small beacon of hope in the encroaching darkness. They spoke little, their words carefully chosen, each syllable carrying the weight of their shared experience. The focus was not on their losses but on the mission that remained.

Brother Thomas, their de facto leader now, addressed them. "Brothers," he began, his voice hoarse, "we have suffered a great loss. But our mission is not complete. The legacy of the Templar Order, the safeguarding of our sacred trust, rests upon our shoulders. We have survived the worst that the Inquisitors could throw at us. But our journey is far from over. We must find a way to reach our final destination, to ensure that the secrets entrusted to us are kept safe for all time. Our faith is our strength, our brotherhood is our shield, and the memory of our fallen brothers will fuel our determination."

Their destination lay far to the west, across the rugged, untamed wilderness of Nova Scotia. The route was

treacherous, fraught with peril, and their small band,

depleted by the battle, was vulnerable. They had to replenish their supplies, find safe passage, and conceal their movements from those who would relentlessly pursue them.

They relied on their accumulated knowledge of the land, their skills of survival, and their unwavering belief in the divine protection of their mission.

The days that followed were a grueling test of endurance. They moved through the dense forests, their steps muffled by the fallen leaves, their eyes constantly scanning for any sign of danger. They foraged for food, hunted game, and relied on their ingenuity to overcome the challenges of the unforgiving landscape. The bond between them, already forged in fire, became even stronger under the pressure of their adversity.

They shared their burdens, their fears, and their hopes, ensuring that the spirit of the Order remained intact.

They encountered various obstacles and dangers, from treacherous ravines and rushing rivers to hostile wildlife and the ever-present threat of discovery. But each challenge they faced only strengthened their resolve. They learned to trust their instincts, rely on each other, and adapt to the ever-changing circumstances. The memories of their fallen brethren served as a constant reminder of the stakes involved, pushing them further, driving them to continue their sacred mission.

They discovered hidden caves and secluded valleys, places where they could rest and regroup, concealed from the prying eyes of their enemies. They used their expertise to create new traps and defenses, enhancing the security of their hidden sanctuary. Their knowledge of the terrain, their skill in construction, and their unwavering determination ensured the success of their endeavor.

As they pressed onward, they encountered isolated

settlements, small, dispersed communities living amongst the harsh beauty of the Nova Scotian wilderness. They bartered supplies with the wary locals, exchanging their limited resources for food and provisions. They learned to navigate the complex web of social dynamics in these communities, maintaining a cautious distance while ensuring their needs were met. Their secret remained safe, concealed beneath the veneer of tired travelers seeking passage through the wilderness.

One fateful day, as they were navigating a treacherous mountain pass, they discovered a hidden valley, a natural amphitheater carved from the granite and shielded by towering cliffs. This was their destination, the final resting place for the sacred relics. It was a secluded sanctuary, hidden from the eyes of the world, a testament to their journey and a sanctuary for their sacred legacy.

Here, under the watchful gaze of the towering cliffs and the silent embrace of the ancient forests, they began their final task. They carefully unearthed the sacred relics from their protective containers, and with meticulous care, they placed them in a hidden chamber within the valley. They sealed it with ancient techniques, strengthening the existing traps and defenses, ensuring that the legacy of the Order would remain safe, untouched by the ravages of time and the greedy hands of their enemies.

Their work completed, they gathered for a final prayer, a heartfelt tribute to their fallen brothers, and a silent vow to safeguard their sacred legacy for generations to come. They had survived the relentless pursuit, the brutal battles, the hardships of the unforgiving wilderness. They had fulfilled their sacred trust. The legacy of the Knights Templar, their unwavering faith, and their sacred secrets, would live on, preserved in the heart of the Nova Scotian wilderness, a silent testament to their courage, their dedication, and their enduring faith. The final stand was over, and their legacy was secured. Their journey was finally at an end. But the echoes of their sacrifice, their courage, and their devotion would continue to resonate through the ages, a timeless ballad of faith, brotherhood, and a legacy protected against all odds.

A Pyrrhic Victory

The last rays of the setting sun cast long, skeletal shadows across the clearing, painting the scene in hues of blood orange and bruised purple. The air, thick with the scent of pine and woodsmoke, was heavy with the silence that followed the storm. A storm of steel and fire, a tempest of desperate men fighting for their lives, their faith, their very souls. The ground, once soft earth, was now churned and scarred, a testament to the ferocity of the battle that had raged just hours before. Scattered amongst the fallen trees and broken branches lay the remnants of the conflict:

shattered swords, splintered spears, and the silent, accusing forms of the fallen.

Brother Thomas, his body aching, his spirit weary, surveyed the scene. The victory was undeniable, the Inquisitors'advance had been decisively halted, their relentless pursuit finally broken. But the price... the price had been steep. He ran a hand through his mud-caked hair, the rough texture a stark reminder of the brutal struggle. Around him, the surviving brothers tended to the wounded, their faces grim, their movements efficient and practiced. The air hummed with the low moans of the injured and the hushed prayers of the dying.

Brother Jean-Luc, his arm hanging limp at his side, leaned heavily against a scarred oak. His usually jovial face was pale, his eyes shadowed with exhaustion and pain. He managed a weak smile as Thomas approached. "We held them, Thomas," he rasped, his voice barely a whisper. "We held them."

"Aye, Jean-Luc," Thomas replied, his voice thick with emotion. "We held them. But at what cost?" He gestured towards the makeshift burial mounds they had hastily constructed, each one a silent epitaph to a brother lost.

"Seven brothers... seven...gone." The weight of their sacrifice settled upon him like a physical blow.

The battle had been a maelstrom of chaotic violence. The Inquisitors, fueled by religious zeal and a thirst for

vengeance, had attacked with savage intensity. They had outnumbered the Templars significantly, their ranks swollen with mercenaries and fanatics eager to cleanse the land of these "heretics." The Templars, though outnumbered, had fought with the ferocity of cornered wolves, their training and discipline transforming them into an almost supernatural force. Their faith, their unwavering belief in their sacred mission, had been their shield, their sword, their very

lifeblood.

Brother Guillaume, ever the strategist, had skillfully

orchestrated the defense. He had utilized the terrain to their advantage, using the dense forest as a shield, drawing the Inquisitors into a deadly trap. The ambush had been brutal, a whirlwind of flashing steel and desperate cries. The Templars had fought back to back, shoulder to shoulder, their bond of brotherhood proving as strong as any fortress wall.

But the Inquisitors were relentless. Wave after wave crashed against the Templar lines, fueled by a hatred that seemed to transcend reason. Brother Etienne, the gentle giant of the order, had fallen early in the battle, a victim of a desperate, frenzied attack. His death had been a blow to their morale, a devastating loss that had nearly shattered their resolve. Yet, they had held. They had persevered.

The final assault had come under the cover of darkness, a desperate attempt to overwhelm the weary defenders. But the Templars, their hearts fueled by grief and righteous anger, met the onslaught with grim determination. Brother Giles, a seasoned warrior, had faced down the Inquisitor's leader, a hulking brute named Sir Reginald, in a duel that had been as brutal as it was brief. Giles, with a final, desperate lunge, had driven his sword through the Inquisitor's heart, bringing an end to the onslaught. But his victory had been pyrrhic; he had collapsed moments later, a mortal wound hidden beneath his armor.

As the last of the Inquisitors retreated, leaving behind a trail of their dead and wounded, a heavy silence descended upon the clearing. The victory was bittersweet, a pyrrhic triumph stained with the blood of their fallen brothers. Their mission was accomplished, their secrets secured, but the cost had been almost unbearable. The echoes of the battle still

lingered in the air, a ghostly chorus of screams and prayers, a testament to the brutal realities of their struggle for survival.

The brothers, their bodies battered, their spirits bruised, began the grim task of tending to the wounded, a solemn ritual performed in the fading light. Brother Thomas, his heart heavy with sorrow, moved amongst them, offering what comfort he could. He felt a deep sense of loss, the weight of his responsibility pressing heavily upon him. He had led these men into battle, and many had paid the ultimate price.

As the night deepened, the brothers gathered around a crackling fire, the flames casting flickering shadows upon their weary faces. The air was filled with the silence of shared grief, broken only by the occasional sigh or whispered prayer. They had survived, but the battle had left its scars, both physical and emotional. The memory of their fallen brothers would remain a constant reminder of the sacrifices made, a bond that would forever link them.

The next morning, the surviving brothers assembled for a final prayer, a tribute to their fallen comrades, their voices hoarse with sorrow, their eyes glistening with unshed tears.

They committed their brothers' bodies to the earth, their silent prayers mingling with the rustling of leaves and the song of the birds. The ritual concluded with a solemn vow, a pledge to continue their sacred mission, to protect the legacy of the Knights Templar, and to honor the memory of those who had given their lives to ensure its survival.

The task of burying their dead was a solemn and

heartbreaking ritual. Each grave was marked with a simple wooden cross, a poignant reminder of the lives lost and the sacrifice made. The silence was profound, broken only by the soft sounds of the earth settling over the fallen, a quiet requiem for warriors who had fought with unwavering faith and courage.

As the sun climbed higher in the sky, casting its golden rays across the landscape, the surviving brothers began to prepare for their departure. Their journey was far from over, the trials and tribulations they faced were still ahead of them. But as they looked upon the graves of their fallen brothers, they found a renewed resolve, their determination hardened by the memory of those they had lost.

The weight of their victory was immense, pressing down upon them like a suffocating blanket. They had won the battle, but the war was far from over. The legacy of the Knights Templar, their sacred mission, their very existence, was still under threat. The journey ahead would be treacherous, fraught with danger, but they would persevere, driven by faith, fueled by the memory of their fallen brothers, and bound together by the unbreakable bond of brotherhood. The pyrrhic victory had left its mark, a deep and lasting wound upon their souls, but they would carry on, their resolve strengthened by their sacrifice, their hearts heavy but their spirits unyielding. Their journey was not over, it had only just begun.

The Passing of the Torch

The biting Nova Scotian wind whipped through the sparse trees, carrying with it the scent of pine and the distant cry of a hawk. The small, hastily constructed shelters huddled together, offering meager protection against the elements.

Inside one of these shelters, a flickering fire cast dancing shadows on the faces of the remaining Knights Templar.

Their numbers, once a proud legion, were now a mere handful, their armor bearing the scars of countless battles, their faces etched with the lines of hardship and loss. Yet, in their eyes, a stubborn ember of faith still glowed. They were not broken. They were not defeated. They were survivors.

Brother Thomas, his hair now streaked with grey, his shoulders stooped under the weight of years and sorrow, held a worn leather-bound book. Its pages, filled with the ancient wisdom and rituals of the Templar Order, were brittle with age, yet their contents remained vibrant, a testament to the enduring spirit of their brotherhood. He looked at the young faces gathered around him – the sons and grandsons of fallen brothers, who had grown up in the shadow of the persecution and the flight from their homeland. These were the future of the Order, the inheritors of a legacy built on faith, courage, and unwavering loyalty.

"For generations," Brother Thomas's voice, though raspy with age, carried a strength that resonated deep within the hearts of the young men, "our Order has guarded the secrets of our faith, the mysteries of our past. Today, that responsibility passes to you. We have protected the relics entrusted to us, not for ourselves, but for the sake of

Christendom, for the preservation of our sacred heritage." He carefully traced a finger across a faded illustration in the book, a depiction of the Holy Grail, a symbol of faith and hope that had guided them through their darkest hours.

"The world outside knows little of our struggles, of our sacrifices. They see only the shadows cast by the Papal decree, the whispers of heresy and conspiracy. But we know the truth. We know the value of our faith, the power of our unity, the unwavering bond that binds us together." He paused, his eyes searching the faces of his listeners, gauging their understanding, their commitment.

The young men, many of whom had barely known a world outside the harsh wilderness of Nova Scotia, nodded solemnly. They had inherited not only the mantle of the Templar Order but also its burden of secrecy, its duty of preservation. They understood the precariousness of their position, the constant threat of discovery and persecution. Yet, they also understood the profound significance of their heritage. They were the guardians of a legacy, the keepers of a flame that had burned for centuries, a flame that would not be extinguished easily.

Brother Thomas then meticulously outlined the intricate network of hidden passages, booby traps, and secret codes that protected their sanctuary and the relics within. He described the location of the vault with precise detail, emphasizing the importance of preserving its secrecy. Each young man diligently copied the details into their own notebooks, their hands trembling slightly with a mix of excitement and solemn responsibility. He instructed them on the proper rituals and prayers, reminding them of the sacred significance of the artifacts and the importance of their role as guardians.

He also explained the intricate communication network they had established with scattered remnants of the Order, ensuring that their knowledge and beliefs would not vanish, that the flame of their faith would continue to burn brightly, even in the most remote corners of the world. This network, built on trust and secrecy, relied on coded messages, carefully chosen messengers, and pre-arranged rendezvous points. It was a fragile system, vulnerable to betrayal, yet vital for their survival. Brother Thomas emphasized the importance of vigilance, urging them to always be wary of potential threats and to rely only on those they could

completely trust.

He spoke of the sacrifices that their ancestors had made, of the blood that had been spilled in defense of their faith and the pursuit of justice. He reminded them of the persecution they had faced, the relentless pursuit by the Inquisition, the relentless betrayal that had nearly broken their ranks. Yet, through it all, the Order had endured. Their faith, their courage, their unbreakable bond of brotherhood – these were the pillars that had supported them through their darkest hours.

"Our strength does not lie in numbers, but in our unwavering faith and devotion to the sacred trust that has been bestowed upon us," Brother Thomas said, his voice gaining strength.

"We have faced immense hardship, and we have emerged victorious. We have overcome insurmountable obstacles, and we will continue to do so. Let our legacy be one of

perseverance, of resilience, of unwavering loyalty to God and to each other."

The passing of the torch was not merely a symbolic act; it was a profound transfer of responsibility, a solemn pledge of loyalty, a testament to the enduring spirit of the Templar Order. It was a promise made in the face of adversity, a commitment to safeguarding a legacy that extended far beyond the confines of their humble shelter, a legacy that would echo through the ages.

As the sun dipped below the horizon, casting long shadows across the snow-covered ground, Brother Thomas concluded his instruction. He placed his hand on the head of the eldest of the young men, a quiet but determined youth named Jean-Luc. "The future of our Order rests in your hands, Jean-Luc," he said, his voice filled with a mixture of sorrow and hope. "Guide your brothers, protect our legacy, and never forget the sacred trust that has been bestowed upon you."

Jean-Luc, his eyes filled with a newfound determination, nodded solemnly. He accepted the mantle of leadership, the weight of responsibility settling upon his young shoulders.

The passing of the torch was complete. The legacy of the Knights Templar, though scarred and diminished, lived on. It lived on in the unwavering faith of the surviving knights, in the strength of their bonds, and in the quiet determination of the young men who would carry their legacy into the future.

The following weeks were spent in meticulous preparation. The surviving Templars, guided by Jean-Luc, consolidated their resources, refined their defensive strategies, and established a more permanent settlement. They worked tirelessly, their hands calloused and blistered, their bodies weary from the relentless labor. Yet, they worked with a renewed sense of purpose, a shared commitment to the preservation of their Order and the protection of their sacred treasure.

They established a system of rotating patrols, ensuring constant vigilance against potential threats. They improved their communication network, ensuring that news and supplies could reach them even in the most isolated regions. They further refined the booby traps and security measures protecting their sanctuary, turning their hidden refuge into an almost impenetrable fortress. They also focused on teaching the young men the skills necessary to survive in this harsh environment, to hunt, to fish, to build, and to defend themselves. The old ways were preserved, blending seamlessly with the innovative strategies adapted to their new circumstances.

The older Templars shared their knowledge and wisdom, imparting not just practical skills but also the spiritual

teachings and the historical context of their Order, providing an understanding of the deep-rooted legacy they were entrusted to safeguard. They also instilled in them the principles of loyalty, discipline, and selflessness – the very foundation upon which the Templar Order had been built.

Despite their losses, the surviving Templars emerged from this period stronger, more united, and more determined than ever. The passing of the torch had not only transferred knowledge and responsibility; it had also ignited a new flame of hope and resilience, a testament to the enduring spirit of their Order and the strength of their faith. The Templars of Nova Scotia were not just survivors; they were the embodiment of resilience, a beacon of hope in the darkness, a testament to the enduring legacy of the Knights Templar. Their story, though shrouded in secrecy, would continue to echo through time, a powerful reminder of the strength of faith, courage, and unwavering loyalty. The legacy lived on, passed from generation to generation, a testament to the enduring spirit of an Order that refused to surrender its sacred trust.

Secrecy and Survival

The harsh Nova Scotian winter tested the mettle of the

remaining Templars. Snow, driven by relentless winds, piled high against their rudimentary shelters, threatening to bury them alive. Food was scarce, hunted mostly by small bands, their meager rations stretched to their limits. Yet, even amidst this stark landscape, the Knights found a grim satisfaction in their self-imposed isolation. Their secrecy was paramount, a shield against the long arm of the papal decree and the avarice of those who would seek to plunder their sacred trust. Brother Thomas, his face weathered and lined, but his eyes still sharp and keen, oversaw the construction of a complex system of hidden passages and tunnels leading to the chamber where the relics were concealed. These weren't just simple burrows; they were intricate engineering marvels, testament to the Templars' skills as builders and warriors.

The entrance, concealed behind a cascading waterfall, was ingeniously disguised, blending seamlessly with the natural landscape. Layers of deceptive pathways, booby-trapped with ingenious mechanisms, protected the inner sanctum.

Pressure plates triggered sharpened stakes, hidden pits

yawned with lethal depths, and cleverly concealed tripwires sent heavy rocks tumbling from above. Brother Giles, a master craftsman before his life as a Templar, had

meticulously designed these defenses, ensuring that any intruders would face a harrowing and potentially fatal

challenge. The knowledge of the traps' locations was passed down only through meticulously crafted maps, written in a secret Templar cipher, held by only a select few, each copy uniquely marked with invisible ink for verification and authentication. Brother Etienne, a scholar and codebreaker of unparalleled skill, created a series of puzzles and ciphers, adding additional layers of protection to the treasure's location.

The relics themselves were housed within a hidden chamber deep within the earth, surrounded by layers of sturdy oak and reinforced stone. The air within was dry and cool, ensuring the preservation of the holy artifacts—a fragment of the True Cross, a chalice rumored to have been used by Christ, and several scrolls containing ancient Templar knowledge and prophecies. These sacred objects, imbued with centuries of faith and history, held a power that transcended their

material form. They were more than just relics; they were symbols of faith, resilience, and the enduring spirit of the Order. Protecting them was their sacred duty, a burden they bore with unwavering resolve.

Their daily routine was a blend of rigorous training,

maintaining their defenses, and praying. The days were spent hunting, gathering firewood, and tending to their shelters, a constant struggle for survival against the unforgiving wilderness. The nights were filled with the murmur of prayers, the sharing of stories from their past, and the constant vigilance that came with living in hiding. Each Templar had his assigned role, their skills honed through years of experience within the Order. They were warriors, builders, scholars, and priests, all united by their shared faith and their dedication to preserving their legacy.

The secrecy extended beyond their physical defenses. They spoke in hushed tones, using coded language to avoid revealing their true identities or the location of their sanctuary. They avoided any contact with outsiders, their interactions limited to occasional silent trades with local indigenous people. This cautious approach did not stem from fear or weakness; it was born of necessity and the profound understanding that their survival depended on their ability to remain hidden. These weren't mere precautions; they were critical aspects of their daily existence.

One evening, around a crackling fire, Brother Thomas, now the de facto leader of the group, addressed his brothers. His voice, though weary, held a firm resolve. "Our legacy is not just about the treasures we safeguard," he said, his gaze sweeping over their faces. "It's about the values we embody—faith, courage, loyalty, and the unwavering pursuit of justice." His words resonated deeply within the hearts of his brethren. Their fight was not merely about survival; it was about perpetuating the ideals that had defined the Order for centuries. It was about safeguarding a way of life, a set of beliefs, that they would not allow to be extinguished. Their existence, lived in secrecy, was a testament to the perseverance of faith in the face of adversity.

The years unfolded like the changing seasons, each bringing new challenges and renewed resolve. The harshness of the wilderness forged them into a more resilient band, their bond stronger than any physical defense. They shared their

burdens, mourned their losses, and celebrated the small victories that punctuated their lives. The indigenous peoples, initially wary, gradually came to accept the Templars' presence, a silent understanding evolving between two vastly different cultures. This unexpected alliance provided a fragile source of support, a delicate balance of trust that was built on mutual respect and shared necessities, a testament to their resilience and their capacity to adapt. Though isolated, they were not alone.

The threat of discovery, however, remained ever-present.

Rumours travelled, whispers of surviving Templars,

shadowy figures seeking wealth and power. The Templars remained vigilant, refining their defenses and sharpening their skills. They knew that their secret could not be kept forever. Sooner or later, the world would learn of their existence. But when that day came, they would be prepared.

They were not merely survivors, they were guardians of a legacy that deserved to endure. Their existence in the harsh, unforgiving landscape of Nova Scotia was a testament to the resilience of the human spirit, a reminder that even in the face of overwhelming odds, faith and unwavering loyalty could overcome any adversity.

One day, a young boy, lost and alone, stumbled upon the hidden entrance to their sanctuary. Brother Jean-Luc, ever watchful, found him huddled beneath the waterfall, shivering and afraid. Initially, hesitation consumed them. The boy, an innocent child, represented a risk to their secrecy. But his helplessness tugged at their compassion. They took him in, providing him with shelter, food, and warmth. His presence stirred a sense of hope within their secluded existence. The boy, named Elias, unknowingly became a symbol of their enduring legacy, a reminder that even amidst secrecy and survival, humanity persevered. His presence instilled a renewed sense of purpose, strengthening the bonds between them. His innocence challenged their isolation, creating a powerful bridge between their clandestine world and the outside world. They taught him their skills, instilled their values, and unintentionally created a link to a future beyond their current existence. He became more than just a child; he became the embodiment of the enduring legacy of the

Knights Templar, a symbol of hope, resilience, and the

unbreakable bonds of brotherhood. His presence transformed their secluded existence, injecting a vibrant current of life into their guarded world.

The legacy of the Templars, once a powerful order, lived on, not in grand castles or opulent halls, but in the hearts of a handful of men and a young boy, hidden away in the

unforgiving wilderness of Nova Scotia. Their survival was a testament to the enduring power of faith, the resilience of the human spirit, and the unwavering strength of brotherhood. They lived in secrecy, but their spirit burned bright, a beacon of hope in the face of adversity. Their story, a tale of survival and secrecy, would ultimately transform from a whisper to a resounding echo, as Elias grew into a man, carrying the torch of their legacy forward.

A New Beginning

The spring thaw arrived slowly, reluctantly, as if hesitant to unveil the harsh beauty of the Nova Scotian wilderness. The melting snow revealed a landscape both desolate and breathtaking – a tapestry of dark evergreens, glistening streams, and rocky outcroppings that clawed at the sky. For the surviving Templars, it marked not just the end of a brutal winter, but the beginning of a new chapter, a new life forged in the crucible of hardship and loss. Brother Thomas, his gaze sweeping across the valley, felt a profound sense of melancholy mingled with a cautious optimism. Their

immediate survival was secured, for now. The hidden

chamber, a testament to their engineering prowess and

unwavering faith, remained undisturbed, a silent guardian of their sacred legacy.

The rudimentary shelters, hastily constructed during the frantic escape from the clutches of the Inquisition, were slowly being replaced with more permanent structures. Their skills as builders, honed over years of constructing fortresses and churches, allowed them to create sturdy dwellings from locally sourced timber and stone, blending seamlessly with the rugged landscape. The young Elias, no longer just a boy but a burgeoning young man, proved remarkably adept at many tasks. His quick mind and tireless energy were invaluable. He learned from the experienced knights, absorbing their knowledge of weaponry, construction, and survival techniques with an eagerness that touched their hearts, reminding them of the future they were striving to build.

The hunt provided sustenance, but it was a grueling pursuit. The bounty of the forest, once abundant, felt surprisingly scarce under their ever-increasing demands. Brother Giles, a seasoned hunter before their exile, taught Elias the art of tracking, the subtle signs of animal movement, and the importance of patience and stealth. Elias's quick wit and sharp eyes, honed by years spent observing the details of their hidden life, quickly made him a valuable asset to the hunting parties. They supplemented their diet with wild berries and edible plants, their knowledge gained from studying ancient texts and careful observation of the local flora. The knowledge of such things had proven far more vital than anyone anticipated when they had first fled Europe.

Their lives were a constant vigilance, a perpetual balancing act between survival and secrecy. The fear of discovery remained a palpable presence, a shadow that clung to them even in the relative isolation of the wilderness. Every rustle in the leaves, every unfamiliar bird call, sent shivers of apprehension down their spines. They had established a network of lookouts and patrols, each member acutely aware of the potential threat. Their faith, once a source of comfort and strength, now felt like a burden, a secret that could condemn them to an even crueler fate than they had already escaped.

Brother Thomas, however, remained steadfast in his faith and their mission. He held the hope that one day, the truth about the Templars would be revealed, and their legacy would be vindicated. The relics they guarded were not just holy objects; they represented the order's enduring spirit, their unwavering belief in God and their commitment to protecting the Holy Land. He knew that their existence, hidden and cloaked in secrecy, was far more than just survival. It was about preserving a testament to their unwavering loyalty and sacrifice. The hope of redemption drove them, urging them towards the future they so desperately sought.

Evenings were spent around a crackling fire, sharing stories of the past, and discussing plans for the future. The tales of their glorious campaigns in the Holy Land were juxtaposed with the harrowing experiences of their flight and subsequent escape. These narratives served as a binding force, reinforcing their bonds of brotherhood in the face of isolation and adversity. They were not merely surviving; they were creating a new life, a new community, born out of shared trauma and unwavering resilience.

The young Elias, listening intently to these stories, felt the weight of their legacy upon his shoulders. He understood that he was not simply a boy who had escaped the carnage of a collapsed order. He was a custodian of a sacred trust, inheritor of a history both magnificent and tragic. He yearned to learn more, not just the practical skills necessary for survival, but the history and beliefs of the Templars, their ideals, and their unyielding faith. The old texts and scrolls, carefully preserved during their arduous journey, became his constant companions. The ancient writings opened his eyes to a world of mysteries and intrigue, illuminating the organization's secrets and hidden purposes, filling him with an ambition to one day restore his lineage's honor.

One evening, under the silvery glow of the full moon,

Brother Thomas presented Elias with a worn leather-bound book – a copy of the Templar Rule. It was more than just a set of guidelines; it was a testament to the order's principles, its values, and its spiritual foundations. "This, Elias," he said, his voice raspy but firm, "is the heart of the Templar order. It is not merely a set of rules but a way of life, a path that transcends hardship and adversity. It is your birthright, your responsibility, and your future." The weight of these words pressed down on Elias, making him feel both the daunting responsibility he bore and the immense pride in his lineage.

As the seasons changed, so did their lives. The harshness of winter gave way to the vibrancy of spring, the abundance of summer, and the golden hues of autumn. With each passing season, they grew stronger, more self-reliant, and more deeply bound together. The forest, once a source of fear and uncertainty, became their sanctuary, their protector, and their provider. They learned to live in harmony with nature, respecting its rhythms and its power. They found solace in their shared experiences, in their unwavering commitment to each other and the sacred legacy they had sworn to uphold. Their new life was far from easy, but it was a life of purpose, a life of dignity, a life dedicated to carrying the flame of the Templars into a new world.

The memory of their past, the pain of their losses, remained a constant presence, but it did not define them. They were survivors, forged in the fires of persecution, and determined to create a future worthy of the sacrifices they had made. They were the last embers of a once-mighty order, flickering but determined to burn brightly until the world was once again ready to accept them. The wind, whispering through the tall pines of the Nova Scotian wilderness, carried their story, a whisper of survival, a testament to resilience, and a promise of the future. The legacy of the Templars lived on, hidden yet indomitable, nurtured in the depths of the

wilderness, ready to rise again, when the time was right.

Hope and Perseverance

The harsh beauty of the Nova Scotian wilderness, once a daunting challenge, now offered a strange solace. The endless expanse of forest, the whispering pines, the unforgiving rocks – they mirrored the resilience that had taken root within the hearts of the surviving Templars.

Brother Thomas, his weathered face etched with the map of their arduous journey, found a strange peace in the rhythm of the land. He watched the sun rise, painting the sky with hues of gold and crimson, a silent testament to the enduring power of creation, a power that had sustained them through

unimaginable trials.

He recalled the horrifying events that had led them to this desolate, yet strangely protective haven. The betrayal in France, the accusations, the tortures, the horrifying spectacle of their brethren being burned at the stake – images that seared themselves onto his memory, refusing to fade. The executioners, the screams, the flames – the very air had seemed to crackle with the malice of their enemies. Yet, even amidst the horrors, a spark of hope had flickered within him, a stubborn refusal to succumb to despair. That spark, he knew, was shared by his brothers.

They had clung to their faith, a beacon in the darkness. Their prayers, whispered in the dead of night, amidst the chilling winds of the Atlantic, were not mere pleas for salvation, but affirmations of their unwavering belief in God's plan,

however inscrutable it might seem. Their faith, honed by adversity, had become a shield, protecting them from the corrosive effects of despair. It was a faith that sustained them through the endless days of travel, through the gnawing hunger and the biting cold, through the constant fear of discovery.

The sacred relics they carried, hidden within the earth, were not merely objects of religious significance; they were symbols of their enduring legacy, a tangible representation of their commitment to preserving the Templar order. The meticulous construction of their hidden chamber, a testament to their skills and ingenuity, mirrored their determination to protect their sacred trust. They had worked tirelessly, their hands blistered and sore, driven by a single purpose: to ensure the survival of their order, to preserve the legacy of the Knights Templar for future generations.

Brother Guillaume, ever the pragmatist, had overseen the construction of their rudimentary shelters, ensuring their protection from the elements. His organizational skills, honed over years of managing Templar resources, proved invaluable in their struggle for survival. He had meticulously planned their food stores, allocated tasks, and established a system of watches, ensuring their safety and preparedness for any eventuality. His quiet competence was a calming influence, a source of strength for the others.

Brother Etienne, a man of deep faith and unwavering piety, had become their spiritual guide. His sermons, delivered under the canopy of the ancient forest, were not merely religious pronouncements, but uplifting messages of hope and resilience. He reminded them of the sacrifices made by their brethren, inspiring them to continue their mission, to honor the memory of those who had fallen. His prayers, his words of comfort, his unwavering belief in the divine plan had served as a balm to their wounded spirits.

Their days were filled with the rhythm of survival: gathering firewood, hunting for game, tending to their meager crops, and constantly scanning the horizon for signs of intruders. Yet, even amidst these arduous tasks, a sense of camaraderie had grown among them. Their shared experiences, their common purpose, had forged a bond of brotherhood that was stronger than steel. They shared stories of their past lives, of battles fought and victories won, of the glory days of the Templar Order before the devastating decree of Clement V. They also shared their dreams of the future, of the day when they could emerge from their self-imposed exile and rebuild the order.

The nights, however, were often fraught with anxiety. The shadows seemed to dance and writhe, their shapes morphing into monstrous figures, reminding them of the ever-present danger. The constant threat of discovery kept them on edge.

They slept lightly, their senses perpetually alert, ready to spring into action at the slightest sound or movement. Their weapons, carefully cleaned and oiled, were always within reach.

Despite the harsh realities of their existence, they found moments of joy and tranquility. They shared laughter around the flickering firelight, telling tales and jokes to lift their spirits. They watched the stars, their brilliance piercing through the inky blackness of the night, reminding them of the vastness and the beauty of the universe, a beauty that transcended their suffering.

They had faced unimaginable losses, yet their spirit

remained unbroken. They had been hunted, persecuted, and condemned, yet they had survived. Their resilience, their unwavering faith, their unyielding hope – these were their most valuable assets. They were not merely surviving; they were persevering, building a new life from the ashes of the old, creating a future worthy of their past.

The legacy of the Templars, once thought to be extinguished, was not only preserved; it was being rekindled, burning brightly in the hearts of these courageous men. Their secret mission, the protection of their sacred treasures, was more than just a task; it was a testament to their faith, their hope, and their enduring perseverance. They were the last embers of a once mighty order, but those embers were far from extinguished; they were burning with a fierce intensity, ready to ignite a new flame, when the time was right.

The wilderness, once a harsh and unforgiving mistress, had become their protector, their sanctuary. It had tested them, pushed them to their limits, yet it had also nurtured them, providing them with the sustenance they needed to survive and the solitude they needed to reflect. The silence of the forest, the whispers of the wind, the gentle murmur of the streams – these were their companions, their solace, their constant reminders that even in the darkest of times, hope could endure. And endure it did, within the hearts of the last Templars, a beacon of faith in the face of unimaginable adversity. Their story was one of survival, of perseverance, a testament to the indomitable human spirit, fueled by

unwavering belief and a sacred mission. It was a story that would resonate through time, a whisper of hope carried on the winds of the Nova Scotian wilderness. It was a story yet to be fully told, a legacy waiting to be revealed. The wind, rustling through the pines, carried the promise of their future, a future born from the ashes of their past, a future forged in the crucible of faith and perseverance. The legacy lived on, hidden, yet indomitable, a testament to the enduring power of hope. The Templars' story, their struggle, their faith, their survival, was not just their own; it was a story for all those who had ever faced seemingly insurmountable odds, a testament to the enduring strength of the human spirit. Their story was a legacy, a testament to the unwavering power of faith and the indomitable spirit of perseverance. The wilderness held their secret, but their spirit echoed through the ages.

The Enduring Faith

The gnawing hunger had become a familiar companion, a constant reminder of their precarious existence. Yet, it was not the physical pangs that weighed most heavily on Brother Thomas's soul, but the gnawing uncertainty of their future.

The harsh beauty of Nova Scotia, initially a formidable obstacle, had become a grudging ally, its unforgiving terrain a mirror of their own resilience. They had built shelters from the fallen timber, their hands calloused and blistered, their bodies lean and hard. The land, once a symbol of their isolation, now represented their sanctuary, a refuge from the relentless pursuit of their enemies.

Brother Jean-Luc, ever the pragmatist, focused on the

practicalities of survival. He had a keen eye for edible plants and fungi, his knowledge proving invaluable in sustaining their dwindling supplies. He meticulously taught the others his skills, his patience unwavering despite the setbacks and frustrations. He believed their survival depended not only on their faith but on their ability to adapt to this new, challenging world. His quiet determination was a constant source of strength, a reassurance that even amidst the wilderness's unforgiving embrace, they could prevail.

Their days were filled with a monotonous rhythm: the

foraging for food, the tending of meager gardens they had painstakingly cleared from the dense undergrowth, the constant vigilance against any potential threat. Nights were spent huddled around meager fires, their stories of the past echoing in the crackling flames, a testament to their shared history, their brotherhood forged in the crucible of adversity.

These narratives, shared under the watchful gaze of the starlit sky, were more than just reminiscences; they were acts of faith, reaffirming their identity, their purpose, their enduring hope.

The relics, carefully hidden deep within the earth, remained their most precious burden. The precise location, known only to a select few, was guarded with an almost religious zeal. The booby traps, cunningly devised, were a testament to their ingenuity, a desperate measure to protect their sacred legacy from those who would desecrate it. Brother Geoffroy, a master craftsman even in this new setting, was responsible for their creation, his skill honed over years of service to the order. Each trap was a reflection of their unwavering determination, a symbol of their resistance against the forces that had sought to destroy them.

Their faith, once tested and shaken, had become a bedrock of their existence. The daily prayers, whispered in the solitude of the forest, were not mere rituals, but affirmations of their unwavering belief. They found solace in the quiet communion with nature, in the majestic expanse of the ocean, and in the towering presence of the ancient trees. Their spirituality, once tied to the grandeur of the Holy Land, had adapted, finding expression in the raw beauty of their new surroundings. It was a faith honed by adversity, refined by hardship, strengthened by their shared struggles.

The silence of the forest was not empty; it was alive with the whispers of their enduring faith. The wind carried their prayers, their hopes, their silent vows. The rustling leaves seemed to murmur their stories, a testament to their perseverance. The crashing waves, the soaring eagles, the rustling pines – all bore witness to their unwavering spirit, a silent symphony of resilience and faith.

One evening, as Brother Thomas watched the sun dip below the horizon, casting long shadows across the forest floor, he

Reflected on their journey. The memory of the condemnation, the betrayal, the brutal persecution, still sent a shiver down his spine. But there was also a sense of peace, a quiet acceptance of their fate. They had escaped the clutches of their enemies, but their struggle was far from over. The wilderness was their sanctuary, but it was also their challenge, a relentless test of their endurance.

The weight of their secret, the burden of their legacy, was immense. But it was a burden they carried with pride, a responsibility they would not forsake. Their survival was not merely a matter of physical endurance; it was a testament to their unshakeable faith, a beacon of hope in the face of overwhelming adversity. Their story was a testament to the enduring power of the human spirit, the capacity for resilience in the face of unimaginable loss and persecution. They were the last of their kind, but their legacy would live on, a silent whisper carried on the wind, a testament to the enduring flame of faith.

The stories they shared around the campfire were not only of their past but of their hopes for the future. They spoke of a time when the world might once again understand and accept their order, when their actions would be viewed not through the lens of political intrigue but as an act of unwavering devotion. This hope, this belief in a better future, served as a powerful motivator, helping them navigate the daily challenges of their existence.

Brother Etienne, the youngest of the group, often spoke of the children they would one day raise, children who would know peace and security, untouched by the hatred and persecution that had marked their lives. This vision of a future generation, free from the shadows of their past, offered a sense of purpose that transcended their immediate survival. It was a future they were fighting for, a legacy they were striving to create, a testament to their unwavering faith in the enduring power of hope.

The nights were filled with quiet reflection, moments of introspection when they would examine their faith, their beliefs, and their purpose. The vastness of the Nova Scotian landscape seemed to amplify their thoughts, allowing them to contemplate the profound implications of their choices, their sacrifices, and the enduring nature of their faith. It was a faith that transcended the boundaries of time and space, a faith that connected them to a larger purpose, a purpose beyond their own mortal existence.

Brother Guillaume, a scholar by nature, would spend hours poring over ancient texts, searching for answers, seeking wisdom, seeking guidance in the face of the unknown. His studies became a form of solace, a way to connect with the past and to reaffirm their connection to the larger history of their order. His research also provided insights into the local flora and fauna, enhancing their survival skills and further integrating them into their new environment.

Their faith was not passive; it was active, dynamic, and evolving. It was a faith that sustained them in their darkest moments, provided them with the strength to overcome seemingly insurmountable obstacles, and inspired them to create a new life in the face of unimaginable adversity. It was a testament to the human spirit's enduring capacity for hope, resilience, and faith even when facing extinction.

They continued to pray, to reflect, to share their stories, to pass on their wisdom and their faith to each other. Their resilience was a testament to their shared history, their unwavering faith, and their enduring bonds of brotherhood. It was not only their faith that kept them going, but also the strength they derived from one another, a bond forged in the fires of adversity, a brotherhood that would endure long after their individual struggles had ended.

The harsh beauty of the Nova Scotian wilderness remained a constant challenge, but it also became a source of inspiration. The resilient nature of the land mirrored their own resilience, their capacity to adapt and thrive even in the most challenging circumstances. Their life in this new land was a testament to their strength, their faith, and their enduring brotherhood, a legacy that would continue long after their time.

Their legacy was not just about the treasures they protected, but also about the faith they embodied, the resilience they demonstrated, and the brotherhood they preserved. It was a legacy that would inspire others, a story of perseverance, a testament to the human spirit's capacity to overcome adversity, and a beacon of hope for those who would follow in their footsteps. The whispering pines, the crashing waves, the rugged landscape—all would bear silent witness to their enduring faith, a legacy etched not only in stone, but in the very heart of the Nova Scotian wilderness. Their story was a living testament to the power of faith, a legacy that would resonate through time, a beacon of hope in the darkest of nights. The enduring faith of the Knights Templar, a flickering flame in the face of oblivion, had found a new home, a new life, in the heart of the Nova Scotian wilderness, a legacy waiting to be discovered, a secret guarded by the very land itself.

Modern Discoveries

The whispers of the Knights Templar, once silenced by the brutal hand of the Inquisition, continue to echo through the centuries. Their story, a tapestry woven with threads of faith, courage, and sacrifice, has captivated imaginations for generations. While the official records paint a picture of a suppressed order, shrouded in mystery and condemned to oblivion, the possibility of their survival, and the safeguarding of their sacred treasures, ignites the embers of intrigue. Modern discoveries, however fragmented and debated, offer tantalizing glimpses into the potential truth behind the legends.

One such avenue of exploration lies in the realm of folklore and oral traditions passed down through generations in Nova Scotia. Stories of hidden caves, booby-trapped passages, and mysterious artifacts unearthed by chance have circulated amongst local communities for centuries. These accounts, often dismissed as mere fanciful tales, bear striking

resemblance to the Templar's meticulous methods of

concealment and the strategic locations described in our narrative. While lacking concrete evidence, these oral

histories provide a compelling starting point for further investigation, hinting at a possible connection between the legendary Templar refuge and the whispers circulating within the province's secluded communities. Perhaps, within the narratives of these communities, lies a coded message, a fragmented echo of the Templar's ultimate fate.

Academic research and archaeological investigations have also contributed to the ongoing quest to uncover the Templars' secrets. While no definitive proof of the Knights' hidden treasure has been unearthed, numerous expeditions have focused on areas historically associated with Templar activity in Nova Scotia. The examination of ancient maps, cryptic documents, and the study of unusual geological formations have all yielded intriguing leads, sparking renewed interest in the possibility of undiscovered Templar settlements. The meticulous analysis of these clues often reveals patterns, suggesting a planned and deliberate concealment strategy, reinforcing the idea that the Templars' legacy was not entirely lost to the tides of history.

Furthermore, the discovery of artifacts bearing striking similarities to Templar symbols and iconography in various locations across Nova Scotia further fuels speculation. Though their authenticity and connection to the Templars remain a topic of ongoing debate among historians and archaeologists, these artifacts undeniably add a layer of mystique to the enduring legend. Their presence sparks the imagination, hinting at a hidden history, waiting to be unearthed from beneath layers of time and mystery. These discoveries, though circumstantial, suggest that the Knights Templar's influence extended far beyond the reach of the official records and the relentless pursuit of their enemies.

The search for the Templar treasure has also captivated the attention of amateur treasure hunters and historians alike.

Equipped with advanced technology and historical

knowledge, these individuals have embarked on numerous expeditions, combing through historical maps, analyzing geological formations, and exploring remote regions of Nova Scotia. The sheer tenacity of these efforts underscores the enduring fascination with the Knights Templar's story and the enduring hope that their secrets will one day be revealed.

Each expedition, despite its uncertain outcome, adds to the collective knowledge, refining the parameters of the search, and potentially bringing us closer to unraveling the mystery of their hidden legacy.

However, despite these intriguing leads and persistent searches, the location of the Knights Templar's hidden treasure remains elusive. This persistent mystery serves as a testament to the effectiveness of their concealment techniques and their commitment to safeguarding their sacred legacy. The absence of definitive proof, far from diminishing the story's allure, only serves to amplify the enigma. The unanswered questions, the unconfirmed legends, and the tantalizing glimpses into a hidden history continue to beckon, fueling the persistent search and stimulating the imagination of those who dare to unravel the Templars' last secrets.

The enduring mystery surrounding the Knights Templar and their hidden treasure is not merely a historical puzzle; it represents a deeper exploration of human nature. It speaks to our inherent fascination with secrets, our innate desire to unearth hidden truths, and our fascination with the legacy of power and faith. The Templar's story resonates with us because it embodies themes of courage, faith, and resilience in the face of overwhelming adversity. Their struggle to protect their beliefs and their legacy transcends historical context; it speaks to the universal human experience of fighting for what one believes in, even when facing seemingly insurmountable odds.

Furthermore, the unanswered questions surrounding their ultimate fate and the potential location of their hidden treasures contribute to their enduring mystique. The lack of definitive answers allows for countless interpretations, fostering a rich tapestry of legends and speculation, engaging both historians and the general public alike. The very nature of the mystery, its resistance to easy resolution, allows the story to continually evolve and adapt to the changing perspectives of time. The enigma of the Templars continues to capture the popular imagination, inspiring countless works of fiction, documentaries, and explorations, and prompting us to contemplate the enduring power of faith, resilience, and the mystery of the past.

The legacy of the Knights Templar extends far beyond the confines of history books and archaeological digs. Their story has deeply infiltrated popular culture, serving as

inspiration for countless novels, films, video games, and artistic expressions. Their image as valiant defenders of Christendom, imbued with both piety and martial prowess, has become synonymous with courage, secrecy, and an enduring commitment to a sacred cause. Their influence extends to our current understanding of historical narratives, religious orders, and the power struggles that have shaped the world we know today.

In conclusion, while the precise details of the Knights Templar's final days in Nova Scotia and the exact location of their hidden treasure remain shrouded in mystery, their story continues to resonate with a profound impact. Modern discoveries, fragmented accounts, and enduring legends all contribute to the enduring allure of the Templar legacy. The unanswered questions only serve to strengthen their legend and keep their story alive in the minds and hearts of those who seek to understand the echoes of their past. The story of the Knights Templar is a testament to the enduring power of faith, courage, and the persistent search for truth, even in the face of seemingly insurmountable odds. Their legacy, deeply intertwined with historical fact and enduring myth, will continue to inspire and intrigue for generations to come, forever shaping our understanding of history, faith, and the enduring mystery of the past.

Unanswered Questions

The wind howled a mournful dirge across the bleak Nova Scotian landscape, mirroring the unanswered questions that lingered in the wake of the Templar's desperate flight.

Generations had passed since the last whispers of their

presence faded into the mists of time, leaving behind only fragmented clues and enduring legends. Did they truly find refuge in this unforgiving land? Did they successfully

conceal their sacred treasures, safeguarding them from the avarice of kings and the relentless pursuit of their enemies? The very earth seemed to hold its breath, guarding its secrets with the tenacity of a slumbering dragon.

Historians, archaeologists, and treasure hunters alike have long been captivated by the mystery surrounding the Templars' final days. The official records, meticulously crafted to erase their existence, offer little more than a skeletal outline of their condemnation and subsequent suppression. Yet, whispers of their survival, carried on the wind like the seeds of resilient wildflowers, persist in the folklore of the region. Tales of hidden tunnels, booby-trapped chambers, and ancient symbols etched into the very stones of the Nova Scotian wilderness continue to fuel the imaginations of those who seek to unravel the enigma of the Templars' legacy.

One of the most perplexing questions centers around the nature of the treasures themselves. Were they merely gold and jewels, the spoils of centuries of conquest and pilgrimage? Or did they hold a deeper significance, perhaps containing sacred relics, ancient texts, or knowledge that could rewrite the history of Christendom itself? The very idea that such knowledge could exist, concealed somewhere beneath the unforgiving soil of Nova Scotia, ignites the imagination and fuels the relentless pursuit of those driven by the allure of lost history.

The possibility that the Templars might have established a hidden community, a secret enclave thriving beneath the radar of the outside world, adds another layer to the intricate puzzle. The harsh realities of the Nova Scotian wilderness would have certainly tested their resilience, their faith, and their commitment to secrecy. Did they forge alliances with the indigenous peoples of the land, drawing upon their knowledge and skills to survive and protect their secrets?

Did they adapt to the unfamiliar environment, creating a sustainable community within the shadows of the vast

wilderness? The surviving accounts are scant and unreliable, leaving these questions hanging heavy in the air, begging for answers.

The few surviving documents— fragmented parchments, cryptic maps, and barely legible journals—offer tantalizing glimpses into the Templar's ordeal. These scraps of evidence, often shrouded in allegory and cryptic symbolism, have been scrutinized and debated by experts for centuries. Each newly discovered fragment, however small, generates a flurry of interpretations, further fueling the intrigue and controversy surrounding the Templars' ultimate fate. Even the seemingly insignificant details— a misplaced word, a hastily drawn sketch, an unusually placed symbol — can become the

cornerstone of a new theory, leading researchers down a rabbit hole of historical speculation.

Archaeological investigations have yielded mixed results. Numerous sites have been identified as potential locations of Templar settlements or hidden caches, but conclusive evidence remains elusive. The challenges posed by the harsh Nova Scotian climate, the dense vegetation, and the passage of centuries have proven insurmountable obstacles for even the most determined researchers. Every dig, every

excavation, is a delicate dance between hope and

disappointment, a constant reminder of the elusive nature of the truth they seek.

The legends themselves, passed down through generations, offer a rich tapestry of narratives, each adding its own unique perspective to the ongoing saga. These oral traditions, often embellished and transformed over time, can offer valuable insights into the Templars' experience in Nova Scotia, reflecting the community's perception of their presence and their impact on the local landscape. By studying these narratives, we can gain a deeper understanding of the way in which the memory of the Templars was preserved and transmitted, allowing us to trace the evolution of the legend and to identify the elements that have persisted through time.

Furthermore, the possibility that the Templars' legacy

extends beyond the physical realm also deserves

consideration. Did their profound spiritual beliefs survive the centuries, influencing the religious landscape of Nova Scotia in subtle yet profound ways? Did their unique spiritual practices leave behind traces in the folklore, traditions, or even the architecture of the region? The interconnectedness between spiritual beliefs and material culture is a critical element to consider when examining the legacy of the Templars.

The very ambiguity surrounding the Templars' ultimate fate and the location of their hidden treasures is what makes their story so enduringly captivating. The unanswered questions serve not to diminish their legacy, but rather to amplify it, transforming them from historical figures into timeless enigmas, forever bound to the mystery of their disappearance and the enduring allure of their lost treasures. The lack of definitive answers only enhances the legend, weaving an intricate tapestry of fact and speculation that continues to capture the imaginations of historians, treasure hunters, and anyone fascinated by the enduring power of history and the enduring mystery of the past. The search for the truth continues, driven by the echoes of their past and the enduring hope that one day, the secrets of Nova Scotia's wilderness might finally be revealed. But until then, the whispers of the Templars, carried on the wind and etched in the stones, will continue to resonate, a testament to the enduring power of a legend that refuses to fade. The unanswered questions, in their own way, are the ultimate testament to the lasting power of the Knights Templar.

The Enduring Mystery

The salt spray stung Elias's face as he stared out at the churning Atlantic. He'd spent his life piecing together fragments, whispers carried on the wind, legends mumbled in hushed tones by old fishermen. His grandfather, a man weathered like the ancient stones of the Nova Scotian coast, had spoken of the Templars, not as historical figures, but as almost mythical beings – protectors of a sacred trust, guardians of a secret that defied the passage of centuries.

Elias, a historian by trade, scoffed at the tales at first,

dismissing them as folklore. But the more he delved into the fragmented records, the faded maps, the cryptic symbols etched into forgotten gravestones, the more the whispers transformed into a compelling symphony of unanswered questions.

The official historical record was barren, a stark contrast to the rich tapestry woven by local legend. The Church, ever diligent in controlling its narrative, had ensured the Templars' story was largely erased, replaced by a carefully curated version emphasizing heresy and treachery. Yet, the silence itself spoke volumes. The very absence of definitive answers fueled the flames of speculation, creating an almost magnetic pull towards the unresolved enigma. Were the stories merely fanciful tales designed to entertain weary sailors and superstitious villagers? Or was there a kernel of truth buried beneath layers of myth and exaggeration?

Elias considered the evidence he'd painstakingly collected over decades. There were the unusual geological formations, strangely reminiscent of medieval fortifications, hidden within the dense forests. The oddly precise arrangement of certain stones – too regular, too geometric to be natural.

Then there were the local place names, whispers of

"Templar's Cove," "Knight's Brook," and "Chapel Hill,"echoing like ghostly remnants of a forgotten past. And the artifacts – the occasional worn coin bearing the Templar cross, a fragment of intricately carved stonework discovered during a coastal erosion, a rusted piece of Templar-style weaponry unearthed by a farmer plowing his field. Each find, though seemingly insignificant in isolation, contributed to a growing sense of unease, a confirmation that the

whispers were more than just stories.

He recalled the painstaking work of deciphering the cryptic symbols found etched into a weathered wooden chest, recovered from a submerged wreck off the coast. The symbols, a mix of Latin, Hebrew, and a unique Templar cipher, had initially seemed impenetrable. But after years of dedicated research, consulting with experts in medieval languages and cryptography, he'd managed to unravel a fragment of the message. It spoke of a hidden sanctuary, protected by ancient magic and guarded by intricate traps designed to deter any who would dare to violate its sanctity. The message tantalized, offering a sliver of insight into the Templar's strategy but leaving the most crucial details

shrouded in obscurity. The exact location of this sanctuary, the nature of its treasures, remained tantalizingly elusive.

The allure wasn't just about the potential discovery of untold riches – though the possibility of recovering artifacts of immense historical significance was undeniable. It was about unearthing a lost chapter of history, piecing together the puzzle of a clandestine society that had vanished without a trace, leaving behind only shadows and whispers. It was about understanding their motivations, their beliefs, the reasons that drove them to risk everything to safeguard their sacred trust. Were they simply protecting religious artifacts, as the official narrative suggested? Or was there something far more profound, something more sinister, or perhaps something far more magnificent?

The mystery extended beyond the physical artifacts. The Templars' disappearance, shrouded in secrecy and conflicting accounts, defied easy explanations. The official story, dictated by the Church and powerful monarchs, painted them as heretics, conspirators, and traitors. But Elias found himself increasingly skeptical of this convenient narrative.

Could it be a cover-up, a desperate attempt to erase the memory of a powerful organization that possessed

knowledge and influence that threatened the established order? The questions multiplied exponentially, each answer leading to a dozen more.

He pondered the lives of the individual Templars who had fled to Nova Scotia. What were their names, their stories, their hopes and dreams? Did they find solace and peace in this new land, far from the persecution and bloodshed of Europe? Or did the weight of their past, the burden of their secret, continue to haunt them until their dying breath? He imagined their faces, etched with the weariness of long journeys and the burden of their sacred duty. He pictured them, huddled around flickering candlelight, whispering their prayers, their hopes, and their fears in a language long since lost to the winds of time.

The enduring mystery was not merely about the location of lost treasures, but about the nature of faith, the resilience of the human spirit, and the enduring power of secrets. The Templars, whether driven by faith, ambition, or a combination of both, had chosen to protect their legacy at any cost. Their sacrifice, their cunning, their unwavering dedication to their cause, all contributed to the aura of mystery and intrigue surrounding their story.

The enigma of the Templars was not solely confined to the realm of history and archaeology. It extended into the realm of human psychology, exploring themes of secrecy, loyalty, betrayal, and the enduring power of legend. Their story resonated deeply with those who sought adventure, those fascinated by unsolved mysteries, those captivated by the tantalizing allure of the unknown. The whispers of their existence, like the echoes of distant thunder, continued to reverberate across the centuries, keeping their story alive in the collective consciousness.

Even today, whispers of hidden tunnels, secret chambers, and booby-trapped caches continue to circulate amongst local communities. The stories, passed down through generations, are embellished with each retelling, transforming historical facts into fantastical narratives. But the essence of the tale remains – a band of courageous knights, driven by faith and loyalty, choosing to safeguard their sacred legacy in the face of overwhelming odds.

Elias knew his search was far from over. The fragmented clues, the cryptic symbols, the whispers carried on the wind, all pointed towards a truth that lay buried beneath the unforgiving soil of Nova Scotia. The truth remained elusive, a tantalizing enigma that beckoned him towards the unknown. He felt the pull of the mystery, a call to unravel the secrets of the past, to shed light on the lives and ultimate fate of these forgotten knights, and to bring to light the truth that lay hidden for centuries beneath the wild and windswept shores of Nova Scotia. The search, he knew, would continue, driven by the echoes of the past and the enduring hope that one day, the full story would finally be revealed. The legacy of the Knights Templar, in all its complexity and mystery, would continue to resonate, a testament to the enduring power of legend. The silence of the ages, however, still held its secrets close, promising both the thrill of discovery and the sting of possible disillusionment – the ultimate test for a historian dedicated to unearthing the truth. The wind continued to howl, carrying with it the whispers of a past that refused to remain silent, a past that beckoned Elias towards the heart of the mystery. The search, he knew, was just beginning.

A Lasting Legacy

The wind, a relentless sculptor of the Nova Scotian coast, carried Elias's thoughts back across the centuries. He

pictured them, the Knights Templar, not as the romanticized figures of legend, but as men of flesh and blood, grappling with faith, fear, and the brutal realities of war and betrayal. Their flight from the Holy Land, a desperate gamble against overwhelming odds, painted a vivid picture in his mind. He saw them, weary and wounded, navigating treacherous seas, their hope flickering like a candle flame against the storm.

Their arrival in this unforgiving land, a testament to their resilience and unwavering determination.

The secrecy surrounding their final resting place was a testament to their dedication to preserving their sacred trust.

The booby traps, ingenious and deadly, were not merely defensive mechanisms; they were a chilling expression of their desperation, a last stand against those who sought to exploit their legacy. Elias wondered about the men who devised these elaborate safeguards, the ingenuity fueled by fear, and the profound commitment to their cause.

Their ultimate sacrifice was not just a historical event; it was a narrative interwoven into the very fabric of the Nova Scotian landscape. The echoes of their story whispered through the ancient trees, rustling in the leaves, murmuring in the waves that crashed against the rocky shores. The land itself seemed to hold its breath, a silent witness to their struggle, their faith, and their enduring legacy. He realized that the search wasn't just about locating a treasure; it was about understanding the profound sacrifices made by these men, their enduring faith, and the weight of their secret mission.

Elias's research extended beyond the physical artifacts. He delved into the archives of European monasteries,

deciphering faded manuscripts, poring over ancient maps, and piecing together fragmented chronicles. He discovered that the Templars were more than just warriors; they were scholars, architects, bankers, and diplomats. They were instrumental in the development of early banking systems, financing the Crusades and supporting the growth of European commerce. Their influence extended beyond the battlefield, shaping the political and economic landscape of medieval Europe in profound ways. The accusations levied against them – heresy, idolatry, and devil worship – seemed increasingly unsubstantiated as Elias's research unearthed more information about their true character. The Pope's decree, a political maneuver designed to consolidate power and seize the Templars' immense wealth, cast a long shadow over their story, but also served as a testament to their influence and power.

His investigation took him to unexpected places. He found himself studying illuminated manuscripts in the Vatican Library, discussing cryptic symbols with cryptographers, and collaborating with geologists to understand the geological formations that may have played a role in the Templars' choice of hiding place. The deeper he delved into the mystery, the more he realized that the Templars' legacy extended beyond their earthly existence. Their story had seeped into the popular imagination, fueling countless books, films, and legends. The romanticized image of the Templar knight, a symbol of courage, piety, and unwavering devotion, was both a testament to their enduring legacy and a reminder of the power of mythmaking.

The Templars had become an archetype, a reflection of our collective fascination with secrecy, mystery, and the enduring quest for the sacred. Their story resonated with people across cultures and generations. Their existence was a reminder of the enduring human desire for hidden

knowledge, a yearning for a deeper understanding of the world and our place in it. Elias came to realize that the

Templars' true legacy was not merely a hidden treasure, but the enduring power of their story, their continued relevance in modern popular culture, and the mystery that continued to draw people to unravel their secrets.

He considered the possibility that the allure of the Templar legend wasn't just rooted in historical curiosity but also in our own psychological and spiritual needs. The Templars represented an ideal, a chivalric order that combined martial prowess with spiritual dedication. They embodied a sense of purpose, a belief in a higher calling, and an unwavering commitment to their ideals – ideals that resonated across centuries, speaking to our longing for meaning in a sometimes chaotic world. Their story, therefore, became a testament not only to their historical existence but to the enduring power of myth and the human need to find meaning and purpose in the stories we tell ourselves.

As Elias continued his investigation, he uncovered evidence that the Templars' influence reached far beyond Europe.

Their network of contacts spanned the globe, from the

Middle East to the Far East. He found evidence suggesting they had established trade routes and maintained contact with various communities, exchanging goods and ideas. Their sophisticated organizational structure and their ability to navigate complex political landscapes demonstrated their remarkable diplomatic skills and strategic thinking. This newfound understanding of their global connections shattered the simplistic narrative of a purely European order.

The Templars, it seemed, were far more internationally connected and influential than previously thought.

The implications of his research were immense. It

challenged the traditional historical narratives that had long dominated the portrayal of the Templars, presenting a more nuanced and complex picture of their activities and influence. It highlighted the need to move beyond simplistic labels and embrace a broader perspective that acknowledged their diverse activities and global reach. It also highlighted the ongoing debate over historical interpretations and the role of narrative in shaping our understanding of the past.

Elias's search was a metaphor for the broader human quest for knowledge and meaning. The pursuit of truth, he realized, was often more important than the truth itself. The journey had transformed him, sharpening his perception, honing his skills, and deepening his understanding of the intricate relationship between history, myth, and human experience. The legacy of the Knights Templar, he concluded, was not merely confined to the physical artifacts they left behind but was embedded in the enduring power of their story, a story that continued to inspire, intrigue, and challenge our perceptions of the past. The echoes of their past reverberated through time, reminding us of the enduring human spirit, the quest for meaning, and the power of

legends to shape our understanding of the world.

The search for the Templars' hidden treasure was ultimately a search for something more profound, a search for truth, a search for meaning in a world that often seems devoid of it. And in his search, Elias discovered something unexpected: a profound appreciation for the men who had sought to protect their faith and their legacy, even in the face of unimaginable adversity. Their story, far from being just a historical

footnote, resonated with a timeless significance, reminding us that the echoes of the past can shape our present and guide our future. Their legacy, it seemed, was not to be found only in the ground, but in the very fabric of history itself, in the stories we tell, and in the enduring human desire to unearth truth, however elusive it may be. The wind still howled, but now it carried with it not just the whispers of the past but also the unwavering determination of a historian who had finally understood the true depth and lasting power of the Knights Templar's enduring legacy. The search was over, but the story continued, woven into the very tapestry of history, a testament to faith, courage, and the enduring

human spirit.

Reflections on Faith and Courage

The salt spray kissed Elias's face, mirroring the tears that welled in his eyes. He stood on the windswept cliff, the relentless Atlantic crashing against the rocks below, a

symphony of nature's power echoing the tumultuous history he'd unearthed. The treasure, the physical artifacts of the Templars' faith, were secured, their secrets safely tucked away beneath layers of earth and ingenious traps. But the real treasure, Elias realized, lay not in gold or relics, but in the enduring spirit of those who had come before him. Their faith, tested and refined in the crucible of persecution and exile, had been a beacon guiding them through the darkest of nights.

It wasn't a blind, unquestioning faith, but a living, breathing thing, forged in the fires of adversity. He pictured Brother Thomas, the grizzled veteran of countless battles, his face etched with the scars of war and the unwavering conviction of a man who had seen God's hand in both victory and defeat. Thomas, who had whispered prayers amidst the clash of steel, who had found solace in the sacraments even when facing imminent death. His courage wasn't the bravado of a reckless warrior but the quiet strength born of deep faith and unwavering devotion. It was a courage that whispered of resilience, of a commitment to a higher power that transcended the immediate horrors of the world.

And then there was Brother Jean, the scholar, the keeper of their sacred texts, his mind a repository of knowledge and wisdom. His faith wasn't solely a matter of battlefield bravery, but an intellectual pursuit, a constant seeking of understanding and meaning. He had painstakingly copied ancient texts, preserving the legacy of their order even as their world crumbled around them. His courage was found in the quiet act of preservation, in the unwavering belief that their history, their faith, mattered enough to be saved, even if it meant risking everything. He believed that the power of knowledge was as potent a weapon as any sword.

The journey across the treacherous Atlantic, the harsh reality of a new land, the constant threat of discovery – these trials hadn't broken them. Instead, they had forged them anew.

Their perseverance, their indomitable will to survive, to protect their sacred legacy, was a testament to the power of faith to sustain and empower. They didn't simply endure; they adapted, they built, they created. They carved a new existence from the unforgiving wilderness, a testament to their unwavering determination and their belief in a future worthy of their sacrifice.

Their faith was not a static entity, but a dynamic force

shaping their actions, their decisions, and ultimately, their destiny. It wasn't a shield against the harsh realities of life, but a guiding light, illuminating their path through the darkness. Their courage wasn't born of recklessness but of a profound conviction, a deep-seated understanding of their purpose, their role in the grand tapestry of history. Their perseverance, their unyielding determination, wasn't simply stubbornness, but a testament to their belief in a higher calling, a belief that transcended their individual suffering.

Elias thought of the countless sacrifices made – the battles fought, the losses endured, the betrayals suffered. The story wasn't simply one of survival; it was a story of faith sustaining courage in the face of unimaginable odds, a story of perseverance forging resilience in the face of despair. It was a story of men who, despite the overwhelming adversity, remained steadfast in their belief in a greater purpose. They found strength not in their own might, but in the unwavering conviction that their faith, and the sacred duty entrusted to them, were worth fighting for, dying for, even if their names were destined to be lost to the mists of time. This was not a mere historical anecdote; it was a profound exploration of the human spirit.

The wind whipped at his clothes, a constant reminder of the relentless forces of nature, mirroring the relentless forces that had sought to destroy the Knights Templar. Yet, they had prevailed, not through brute force alone, but through a potent combination of faith, courage, and a remarkable capacity for perseverance. Their legacy lived on, not just in the hidden treasure, but in the enduring echoes of their struggles, their faith, and their unwavering determination to safeguard their beliefs.

The discovery had changed Elias. It wasn't merely the

unearthing of a historical mystery; it was a profound spiritual awakening. He'd come seeking a lost treasure, a tangible artifact of the past. He'd found something far greater, something more valuable: an understanding of the indomitable human spirit, a testament to the power of faith in the face of adversity, a testament to the enduring legacy of the Knights Templar. Their story was more than a historical account; it was a lesson in perseverance, in the resilience of the human soul when faced with impossible odds.

He understood now the depth of their faith, not as a rigid doctrine, but as a living, breathing force that had guided their every step, sustained them through unimaginable hardships, and ultimately, ensured their legacy. It was a faith that inspired courage, not through blind obedience, but through a profound understanding of their purpose, a conviction that transcended their earthly existence. Their courage wasn't the reckless abandon of a warrior, but a quiet strength, born of faith, tested and refined by adversity. It was a courage that whispered of resilience, a quiet strength that echoed through the centuries.

The whispers of their past, once muted by time, were now resonating clearly within him. The weight of their story, once a burden, had become an inspiration, a source of strength and understanding. Their struggles were not just theirs alone; they echoed the struggles of all humanity, the constant battle against adversity, the ongoing search for meaning, the enduring human spirit that refuses to be broken.

Elias looked out at the vast expanse of the ocean, the setting sun painting the sky in hues of orange and purple, a majestic display of nature's beauty, mirroring the enduring beauty of the human spirit. The Knights Templar, he knew, had found solace in their faith, strength in their courage, and resilience in their perseverance. Their legacy was a testament to the enduring human spirit, a message whispered across the ages, a testament to the unwavering power of faith, the quiet strength of courage, and the remarkable capacity of the human spirit to persevere even in the face of overwhelming odds. Their faith had not been a passive acceptance of fate, but an active force shaping their lives, guiding their actions, and ultimately, shaping their legacy.

The echoes of their past resonated not just in the artifacts buried deep beneath the Nova Scotian earth, but in the very fabric of history itself, in the enduring human desire to seek truth, to find meaning, and to persevere in the face of adversity. It was a legacy of courage, faith, and

perseverance, a lesson for all who would follow, a testament to the enduring power of the human spirit, a tale that would continue to be told, echoing through the generations to come. The wind carried their story, a testament to the unwavering spirit of the Knights Templar, a legacy etched not only in the stone, but in the hearts of those who learned to understand their sacrifices and their enduring faith. The story of their flight, their courage, and their faith, was a story of

humanity's unyielding spirit, a story that would continue to resonate, echoing through time. Their legacy was more than relics and treasures; it was a testament to the human capacity for faith, courage, and unwavering perseverance, a lesson learned not in the past, but in the enduring power of their story.

Acknowledgments

The writing of this book has been a journey, and I am deeply grateful to the many individuals who have supported me along the way. First and foremost, I want to thank my family for their unwavering patience and encouragement, especially during those late nights spent hunched over my research and writing. Their love and understanding have been invaluable.

My gratitude also extends to the scholars and historians whose works have illuminated the fascinating world of the Knights Templar and the tumultuous era of the Crusades.

Their meticulous research and insightful analyses have provided the foundation upon which this story is built.

Glossary

This glossary provides definitions for key terms and concepts used in the novel:

Grand Master:

The supreme leader of the Knights Templar.

Preceptory:

A local unit or commandery of the Knights Templar.

Papal Bull:

A formal letter or decree issued by the Pope. **Inquisition:**

A tribunal of the Catholic Church established to suppress heresy.

Relics:

Objects associated with holy figures, often considered sacred.

Micmac:

Indigenous people inhabiting parts of Nova Scotia during the 14th century.